P9-BZH-494

APR   - 2006

UNTIL OUR
LAST EMBRACE

A Sharyn Howard
Mystery

UNTIL OUR LAST EMBRACE

•

Joyce and Jim Lavene

AVALON BOOKS
NEW YORK

© Copyright 2001 by Joyce and Jim Lavene
Library of Congress Catalog Card Number: 2001094758
ISBN 0-8034-9508-0
All rights reserved.
All the characters in this book are fictitious,
and any resemblance to actual persons,
living or dead, is purely coincidental.
Published by Thomas Bouregy & Co., Inc.
160 Madison Avenue, New York, NY 10016

PRINTED IN THE UNITED STATES OF AMERICA
ON ACID-FREE PAPER
BY HADDON CRAFTSMEN, BLOOMSBURG, PENNSYLVANIA

Tell me now you love me
And hold me in your heart
Create a space of tenderness
For when we are apart

Tell me now you love me
So when we both grow old
The fire of your passions
Will keep me from the cold

Tell me now you love me
And live with me in light
So when the aging sun has set
I can face the growing night

—Christopher Lavene

Harmony, NC(AP)—A bear killed and partially ate a man at a campground several miles from a bear viewing area.

The body of George Tully, 41, of New River, Tennessee, was found Saturday at the Run Amuck campground near Harmony, a community in the Uwharrie Mountain Range, about 50 miles from Charlotte. The attack apparently occurred late Friday.

Bruce Bellows, a spokesman for the NC Department of Fish and Game, said he could recall only three cases of bears attacking people and eating them in the past 20 years.

Tully was apparently alone at the campground, sleeping outdoors, with only a tarp for shelter, about three miles from a bear-viewing platform operated by the U.S. Forest Service.

1

Diamond Springs deputy Joe Landers said there had never been a bear attack before in the viewing area or the campground, even though "the tourists have been known to get real close to the bears."

Chapter One

"Sheriff Howard? There has been another one!"

"Another one . . . what?"

"Another camper eaten by a bear!"

"*What?*"

"They found her a short while ago. The medical examiner is on his way up the mountain. Deputy Robinson says the state won't like the publicity."

"Thanks, JP. I'll be right there." Sharyn Howard put down the wrench she was using to try to separate the drainpipe under the kitchen sink. It was Sunday, her day off. She thought she'd be able to get a few things done around the house. It never failed. Those were always the times that something unexpected happened in Diamond Springs.

Sharyn had been the sheriff of Diamond Springs for three years. She was the first woman elected sheriff in the history of the state of North Carolina. Sometimes, she thought those three years must also be the hardest in the town's history. Growth in the county population had brought changes to the area that were unforeseen and not necessarily welcome. Money was tight as the county tried to cover all the needs of the expanding population. Tempers were high as a result. There were no quick, or easy, answers.

"Sharyn?" her mother called as Sharyn was trying to get out from under the sink.

Sharyn hit her head hard on the cabinet and dropped the wrench on her knee. The water pipe, which had resisted all efforts to pull it apart for the past twenty minutes, opened suddenly, showering Sharyn. Her mother's voice was apparently the catalyst. She hadn't needed the wrench after all.

"What in the world are you doing under there? Didn't you remember to turn off the water?" Faye Howard asked imperiously.

Sharyn grabbed the towel she'd planned to use when the pipe opened. It wouldn't do much good. Water was everywhere and she was soaked. She jammed the pipe back together and climbed out from under the sink.

"You're making a mess on the floor, Sharyn!" Her mother reached for another towel to clean up the mess. "What are you doing?"

"Trying to fix the water pipe," Sharyn answered, gingerly touching the sore spot on her head where she'd banged it. It was a good thing she had a hard head. "I turned off the water. This was left in the pipe."

"Why didn't you call Dewey? He could have done that!"

"I thought I'd try it first," Sharyn told her, getting to her feet. "Now, I'm calling Dewey."

"And leaving the mess for me to clean up, I suppose?"

Sharyn sighed. "I'll clean it up when I get back, Mom."

"Back? I suppose someone else died or a store was robbed? Why do these things always happen when I need you here?"

Sharyn looked at her mother in her pretty pink suit. She had a small, pillbox hat sitting at a jaunty angle on her elegantly coiffed head. Hearing her mother say those words took her back. How many times had she heard her say them to her father?

T. Raymond Howard had been a patient, understanding man. His method of dealing with his wife had been to take her in his arms and kiss her, then leave her to it as he went out to work. He'd been the sheriff of Diamond Springs for twenty years until three men, who were robbing a local convenience store, recognized him from his election posters. They'd gunned him down. He was unarmed, wearing his bedroom slippers, as he went out for some milk for coffee one Sunday morning. Sharyn had been elected in his place.

Sharyn frowned at her mother. She didn't have the patience or the relationship with Faye Howard to know what to say to her mother. "I'll call Dewey from the car, Mom. And I'll clean up the mess when I get back. Did you pick up my uniforms?"

Faye Howard smiled and patted her glossy curls. Her face turned a little pink.

"You forgot my uniforms? Mom, I have to go to work!"

"I didn't forget them," her mother protested. "I went by to pick them up. But there was an accident."

"An accident?"

"I was trying out that new cleaners out at the mall. They—uh—made a mistake with your uniforms."

"What kind of mistake?"

"They dyed them blue."

"They dyed them blue?"

"You heard me, Sharyn. There's no good repeating it! They made an honest mistake. If it makes you feel any better, they dyed my new dress, too. That nice green one with the lace and the—"

"Mother!"

"I'm sorry, Sharyn! The cleaners will pay for them.

You'll just have to order new ones." She glanced at her watch. "I'm late, dear. I have to go."

"Lunch with Caison?"

Faye Howard smiled. "Of course." She looked at her oldest daughter. "Sharyn, I know you don't like Caison, but—"

Sharyn turned her head.

"Never mind. I'll see you later, dear." Faye Howard gave up before she started and closed the door quietly behind her.

Sharyn put down the wrench and dried her hands on the towel her mother had pulled out. It wasn't that she didn't like Caison Talbot. Okay, it was that she didn't like Senator Talbot. She didn't like him and she didn't trust him.

She understood that he had been her father's friend and that her mother had known him all of her life. She just didn't want her mother to marry him. But with the engagement set and a party coming up that would include most of the state, it was becoming more and more likely that Faye would marry him. They didn't have a date set for the actual marriage but it was only a matter of time.

Sharyn remembered that they were waiting for her on Diamond Mountain. She changed her clothes, putting on a warm blue sweater and a pair of jeans. She clipped her sheriff's badge to her jacket and pulled on her holster that held her grandfather's service revolver. Her grandfather, Jacob Howard, had been the first elected sheriff in Diamond Springs, fifty years ago.

Sharyn looked at herself in the mirror. She'd cut her copper red, curly hair short again. It was too hard to take care of when it got long. The stylist had cut it shorter than usual. It emphasized her freckles and her blue eyes. She looked a little closer. She was beginning to get a permanent frown line between her brows. She pushed at the wrinkles with her fingers, then frowned and turned away.

She'd gained a few pounds in the past few months since Ernie, her head deputy, had left the department. It seemed like the stress would make her thin but apparently, it didn't work that way. As usual, her body found a way to gain weight. Her uniform normally made her aware of that fact. Now, she felt awkward without it. It might take a week to get a new one. She couldn't hide in the house until that happened. Diamond Springs needed its sheriff. Sometimes, it was an awesome responsibility.

The phone rang in her Jeep as she climbed inside. It was Foster Odom, the new reporter that they'd hired at the *Gazette*. Ever since he'd found her cell phone number, he'd been calling her. It had only been a week but it seemed longer. She was going to have to change her number.

"Heard another person was attacked by a bear on the mountain," he said without bothering to tell her his name. "Care to comment?"

Sharyn started the Jeep. "If you don't stop calling me on this line," she promised, "I'm going to have you picked up for impeding justice."

"How will that look in the paper, Sheriff? We both know you haven't stopped me because the election is next year. You need to be accessible to your voting public."

Sharyn backed out of the drive to the street. "If you want the story, Mr. Odom, you'll have to drive up the mountain just like everyone else." She hung up before he could say anything more. Then she dialed the number for the cell phone company.

Accessibility wasn't one of Sharyn's problems. Everyone knew how to get in touch with her and where she lived. Everyone in town knew her whole life story. She'd grown up in Diamond Springs under the microscope of being the sheriff's daughter. She was used to small-town life.

Her problems were more complex. She was down one deputy since Ernie Watkins had refused to come back to the department after being involved in a murder case last fall. He'd left to be with Annie, his high-school sweetheart. Sharyn didn't blame Annie for not wanting Ernie to put his life on the line anymore. She did wish the couple would work it out so that Ernie could come back to work, even if it was only at the office and not in the field.

Deputy Lennie Albert had been 'transferred' to the DA's office. Assistant District Attorney Michaelson had left after his botched attempt to solve the same murder. It was either that or face a demotion from his irate boss. Lennie didn't have the experience to take his place but the DA found another spot for him. Just as well for her. She would've fired him for going behind her back to report things to the DA and the press.

She'd managed to hire another deputy, JP Santiago, who was working out all right. She had a stack of applicants on her desk that she could talk to about the other vacancy but her heart wasn't in it. She still believed Ernie would come back. He'd been with the department for almost twenty-five years, before her father had been elected sheriff. She trusted him and she needed him on the job.

On the other hand, if she didn't choose another deputy soon, the county commission would probably take away her funding. Then she'd be left with an empty space that the rest of the department had already been struggling to fill. She knew it wasn't fair to the other deputies. She just wanted Ernie back. Putting that thought away from her, she turned up the road that led to the top of Diamond Mountain.

It wasn't hard to find the spot where the victim had been located that morning. There was only one road up the mountain, even though there were various hiking trails and historical sites that splintered away from it. It was February, so there weren't many people camping up there. The mountain was preserved as a wilderness area so it was kept open all year but the winter months were usually quiet.

The Montgomery County emergency helicopter and a sheriff's car were already at the site. Ed and JP waved her down when they saw her Jeep. The ME's car was there with a paramedic unit. There was a sport utility vehicle from the Fish and Wildlife agency and a black sedan with state vehicle plates on it. Sharyn shook her head. It looked like the county Christmas party! She parked next to the paramedic unit and put her cell phone in her pocket. She saw the reporters and the television cameras and took a deep breath.

"Sheriff! Is this another bear attack? What do you think is causing the bears to attack? Is Diamond Springs in any danger from rabid bears?"

"I probably don't know as much about it as all of you right now," Sharyn told them, continuing to walk as the circle of reporters walked with her.

"But you can confirm that there were two bear attacks already this year, can't you, Sheriff? Someone was killed up here by a bear last night, weren't they?"

Sharyn stopped and faced them. "If you'll give me a few minutes to talk with my deputies and go over the scene, I'll get back with you."

"On your word of honor, Sheriff Howard?" Foster Odom, the obnoxious reporter from the *Gazette* asked her, with a twang of sarcasm in his tone.

"On my word of honor," she replied. "Cross my heart."

Some of the other reporters snickered and stared at the new reporter, then they made way for Sharyn to cross the yellow tape that separated them from the victim.

"What happened?" Sharyn asked when she reached the other deputies.

"Darva Richmond," Ed told her, walking up the hill to where the victim was lying on the cold ground. "Name sound familiar?"

Sharyn glanced at her deputy. "A little. What don't I want to know?"

Ed consulted his notebook, then pointed to a man who was standing off to one side. "Donald Richmond. Darva's husband. Beau Richmond's brother."

Sharyn looked at the other man. He was wearing long underwear, boots, and a jacket. He hadn't looked up at them yet. He was staring at the woman on the ground with an expression of horror on his lean face. *Beau Richmond's brother.*

"Nothing like ghosts of the past coming to haunt you," she observed. Beau Richmond had been intimately involved with the last murder they'd had in Diamond Springs. He'd been the victim. "Is this the brother who's caused so much trouble, contesting the will and everything?"

"You got it, Sheriff," Ed told her with a grim smile on his attractive face. He ran his hand through his curly blond hair. "They've only been here a few months from Montana. They live with the widow over at the mansion while he's taking her to court to try to take everything away from her."

"That must be fun," Sharyn remarked.

"Yeah," Ed agreed. "You'd think it would be him dead at the foot of those long stairs in the mansion!"

Sharyn looked around the deserted campground. "What's his story?"

"JP's got that," Ed replied. "Kid's gotta do something, Sheriff."

"Where is he?" she wondered.

"Over there with Nick and his assistant."

"Let's go," Sharyn said, dragging her feet. Her breath frosted before her in the cold air. Just this time last week, there was talk of an early spring. Now, the first few blossoms that had come out on the ornamental trees were withered and brown after the heavy frost last night. It felt more like snow than like spring.

Nick Thomopolis, the county medical examiner, was crouched over the body. His black hair was streaked with white and barely combed. He needed a shave. His face was red from the cold as he examined the body. An avid-looking young woman with purple hair was at his side, greedily taking in everything he was telling her.

A green-faced JP was with them, taking notes. He looked up as Sharyn and Ed approached. He turned his back on the corpse with a grateful expression on his thin face. "Sheriff," he greeted her with a big, lopsided smile. "I'm glad to see you! This is terrible! I've never seen . . . I didn't know a person looked like this when they were eaten."

"That's okay, JP. I'm not looking forward to it either. And Nick loves to make things hard." She raised her voice a little on the last part.

Nick lifted an inquiring coal black brow at her words but didn't stop to look at her. The girl at his side turned her back more firmly to them.

"What do you have so far?" Ed asked the new deputy.

JP took out his notebook. "The bear victim is named Darva Richmond. Her husband," he pointed to the man in the long underwear, "says they were out here camping." He pointed to the small travel trailer. "He says she got up during the night to go to the bathroom because theirs wasn't working in the trailer. He went back to sleep and when he woke up, she was still gone. He got dressed and came out to look for her. He found her here." He pointed to the body, then looked back at Sharyn. "She was short only a few feet from her goal, Sheriff Howard."

Ed frowned thoughtfully. "The bear would've chased her into the bathroom anyway. I don't think that little building would've kept him out."

JP nodded solemnly. "You are probably right, Deputy Robinson, sir."

"Ed," the other deputy said. "Call me Ed."

"Yes, sir!"

Sharyn took a deep breath. "Well, that part was easy. Let's see what Nick has to say."

Nick didn't look up as she approached him. He continued to talk, laying out facts about the body while his student wrote them down in her notebook.

"Good morning, Nick," Sharyn acknowledged him quietly.

"Sheriff!" he said as though he hadn't seen her. "Megan, now you'll see a real professional at work! Move aside and let the sheriff take a look at the body."

Megan popped a bubble with her gum. She moved about six inches from where she had been crouched beside Nick. She looked up at Sharyn and snorted. The nose ring she wore caused the warm air to come out as half circles.

Sharyn huddled in her coat. "I'm the sheriff, not the ME."

"But you *are* the sheriff, Sheriff. Tell us what your take is on this particular body."

Sharyn had never seen a body partially eaten either. It wasn't a pretty sight. She struggled with her revulsion and swallowed hard on the nausea that came up in her throat. Briefly, she recalled meeting Darva Richmond at a party that was given by the county commissioners. She was a beautiful woman, with a vivacious manner, who'd drawn a crowd of admirers that night.

Try as she might, Sharyn couldn't see anything of that woman in this corpse. The face had been badly mauled and the throat was torn open. Some of her fingers were gone and one of her feet. The carnage to the mid-section of her body was awful. She was wearing what was left of a red terry robe and what looked like a blue nightgown. Sharyn struggled for words to describe what she saw in front of her. None came to mind.

"Go get the camera from the car, Megan," Nick finally told his student.

"Professor—"

"Now!"

Megan stood up and groaned a few times but eventually she dragged her feet to the car.

Nick looked at Sharyn. He felt like an idiot. "Are you all right?" He started to put his arm around her shoulders but stifled the gesture quickly. He didn't want to find out what her feelings were about *that*.

Sharyn glanced at him, barely noticing that he was there beside her until he spoke. "Yeah. I'm okay." She managed to smile a little. "I guess I just don't get out enough to know what to expect from a partially eaten body."

"That's right. You missed the first one because you were at that conference."

She nodded and then realized that everyone was looking at her. "Let's do this, Nick."

"Right." He tried to get his scattered thoughts together. "All right. The woman has been dead at least eight hours. There was frost last night and again this morning." He pointed to the woman's clothes. "You can see where the frost is showing twice. She was out here before the first frost around midnight. There's not much blood around her but no drag marks on the ground. Since an animal was involved, we can probably assume she was killed here, like her husband said, trying to get to the portable toilet. The bear probably—er—disposed of the blood."

"Wouldn't she have screamed enough that he would've heard her last night?"

Nick pointed to the throat. "She probably wasn't able to scream. I think this might have been the first blow, although she has a side head wound that might have knocked her out and on the ground before she could yell for help."

"No doubt it was a bear?" she considered.

14   *Joyce and Jim Lavene*

"No doubt. Look at those claw marks and the places where the teeth—" He looked at her and shook his head. "No doubt she was attacked by a bear. I've seen a few others besides the two this year. They don't happen often but they're pretty memorable."

Sharyn nodded and looked at Darva Richmond's picture on her driver's license. She looked at the wedding ring that remained on one of the woman's hands. Her purse was ripped and the contents scattered out around her.

"Wonder why she took her pocketbook with her to the bathroom?" Ed asked.

Nick shrugged. "Don't ask me! Women take them everywhere, don't they?"

Sharyn smiled at him. "Thanks, Nick."

"For what?" he wondered.

"Being here," she responded.

Megan returned with the camera. Nick forced himself to look away from Sharyn's face.

"What's this stuff?" Sharyn asked briefly as she looked at the body one last time. There was a congealed clear substance that was visible around a few of the wounds.

"That's body fluid," Megan told her. "It's frozen from the cold!"

Sharyn looked skeptical. Nick bent his head to look at where she pointed.

"I'm not sure." He took out a swab and placed a sample of the substance in a jar. "I'll let you know. Will the county pay for an autopsy on this?"

"Not unless you see something suspicious without the autopsy. Her death seems pretty straightforward."

"All right. I'll check this stuff out before I release the body to the family. Anything else?" he wondered.

"No, thanks." Sharyn left him and walked towards Darva's husband. "I'm sorry for your loss, Mr. Richmond."

She held out her hand to him. "I'm Sheriff Sharyn Howard."

"I can't believe it," he said in an undertone laced with horror. "Bears don't eat people."

"Sometimes, they do," she assured him. "Let me have a deputy take you home. I don't think you should be driving like this. You can come back for your car and the trailer."

He looked at her with frozen blankness in his eyes. "Where will I go?"

She put a hand on his arm. "You need to go home. I know this is hard, Mr. Richmond. You just need some time."

"Darva?" He nodded at his wife's body without looking at her.

"We'll take care of her for now. Let me find a deputy. Please let me know if there's anything I can do for you."

He didn't respond. Sharyn walked back to JP and asked him to take Donald Richmond home. "I don't think he should be behind the wheel."

"Gladly, Sheriff Howard, ma'am." He bobbed his close-cropped head. "I will take him home."

"Thanks, JP. Sheriff is enough." She joined Ed and the NC Wildlife manager, Bruce Bellows. "Bruce."

"Sheriff." Bruce shook her hand. He put his hands in his jean pockets, the stance emphasizing his fleshy hips and short, stocky legs. "Bad stuff here."

She shivered, thinking about the body. "Yeah. What about the bear? Any way of finding it?"

"I think we can find it." He looked up and nodded. "There's my tracker now."

An older, Native American man stood near the grisly scene, examining the ground. He carried a rifle on his back. His long, iron gray hair swung across his face as he touched the frozen ground.

"I'll introduce you to him," Bruce volunteered.

The three of them joined the man. He was still kneeling on the ground.

"Sam, this is Sheriff Howard and Deputy Robinson. Ed, Sharyn, this is Sam Two Rivers. What do you think, Sam?"

Sam stood up and looked at them. He was at least sixty, maybe older. His tanned face was deeply lined. He looked muscular and solid in his traditional garb. He wore a heavy coat over his brown tunic and loose pants. His black eyes were sharp with dislike and anger. "I think this is stupid."

Bruce grinned at Sharyn and Ed by way of apology. "What do you mean stupid?"

"What do you think stupid means?" He turned to walk away.

"Would you mind explaining to me why it's stupid?" Sharyn asked him.

He glanced back at her. "Come with me."

Sharyn was used to hiking in the Uwharries. She was barely able to keep up. Sam Two Rivers set a grueling pace across the rock and loose shale. He made no exceptions for the fact that there were other people following him. He refused to take the paths that criss-crossed the mountain and almost seemed intent on losing them. Hearing the labored sounds of breathing behind her, Sharyn concentrated on following him. Ed and Bruce would just have to follow the best they could.

The sun was watery and restless, peering down at them through a thick layer of clouds. The air was heavy with precipitation. As they climbed further up the mountain, the ground was covered with sheets of ice, making the trek even more difficult. The bushes were thinner and the trees became scarce. Diamond Mountain was only fifteen hundred feet but sometimes the ascent could be steep.

A doe and a young fawn ran from them, crashing through what cover they could find. The mountain was protected from hunters. The animals were less wary than they might be in the lower woods. The doe waited so long to move that Sharyn wasn't sure if she was going to run or not. A small, red fox poked out its head and took a look at them. Overhead, a brown hawk called out as it searched for food on the ground.

Sharyn wondered how far they were going when Sam Two Rivers finally came to an abrupt halt near the mouth of a cave. She pulled up short to keep from crashing into him. Ed collapsed somewhere behind her while Bruce leaned over, trying to catch his breath.

"Where—where are we?" Bruce wheezed as he spoke.

"Quiet!" Sam hissed.

Sharyn peered through the underbrush and rock beside Sam. She started to speak but he covered her mouth with his hand. Sam's eyes were fierce on her face, warning her not to speak. A big mother black bear came ambling out of the dark cave. Sharyn nodded that she understood and then wondered where Bruce had found this tracker.

A moment later, three cubs followed their mother out of the cave. The mother looked around and sniffed the air but her visitors were downwind. She couldn't detect them. The cubs rolled each other around and played with their mother. The sun broke through the clouds, giving some warmth to the morning chill. The mother persuaded the cubs, still playing with each other, that it was time to visit the river below. They walked away, disappearing into the underbrush.

Sam stared at Sharyn. "Now, do you understand?"

Sharyn faltered, then she shook her head. "No, Sam. That's why you're the expert, I guess."

"This mother is the only one up here right now. The others are still hibernating. She had those cubs to feed. They probably woke early and needed her."

"Are you saying the three of them killed that woman?"

"I'm saying none of them killed her!'

Sharyn had her doubts. "You saw the body, Sam. I don't think that's in question at this point!"

"I'm not saying she didn't gnaw on it some," he argued. "I'm saying she didn't kill the woman. She wouldn't kill a human unless she was too close to her cave and her cubs. Does this look close to you, Sheriff?"

"No," Sharyn admitted. "But they might have come upon her."

"She wouldn't kill."

"Did we ever find the bear that did the first killing?" she asked Bruce.

"We did. Sam trapped it and we sent it to the zoo in Asheboro. It was a male."

"That's another thing," Sam pointed out. "Two different bears killing humans within just a few months of each other? This was a mild winter, Sheriff. One bear might have been aggressive. A female with cubs would only be aggressive if her cubs were threatened. Only *her* tracks were at the scene."

Sharyn looked at him. "But you did just track the bear here, didn't you? This is the bear that mauled Darva Richmond?"

"Yes," he agreed. "But—"

"We can't take a chance that it could happen again. Bruce, see if you can find someone to take her and get her off the mountain. I don't want to have to kill her."

Sharyn turned to go. Ed dusted off his backside and got ready to go with her.

"Wait, Sheriff!" Sam held her back with his hand on her arm. "You don't know what you're doing! Do you know how small the bear population on Diamond Mountain is now? We need every female bear we can find! I was born and raised here. I know this mountain and I know these bears. That other bear was a renegade. This bear stumbled across that woman and messed her up a little but she didn't kill her!"

"I understand your concern for the animals," Sharyn agreed. "And I know it hasn't helped them that we have people living in places that used to be their homes. But they pay me to care about what happens to the people, even if they are in the wrong place at the wrong time."

"I understand, Sheriff," Bruce intervened. "I should be able to find a place for the mother and her cubs."

"At least let me keep the cubs here," Sam pleaded. "They look old enough to be without their mother. Don't send them away because you don't trust her!"

Sharyn sighed. She wasn't prepared to make that judgment. "That's fine with me if you have the permits to keep them. It's up to Bruce."

Bruce shrugged.

Sam nodded. "You can send her away, Sheriff. But that won't solve your murder!"

Sharyn smiled and shook his hand. "Thanks for your help. You won't mind if I hope you're wrong."

Chapter Two

Since JP took the sheriff's car back to town with him, Ed rode with Sharyn. "New uniform, Sheriff?" he wondered with a smile, looking at her jeans.

"No, Ed, and don't give me a hard time about it. The dry cleaner dyed them blue."

"Your uniforms? *All* of them?"

Sharyn shrugged. "My mother took them all to a 'new' dry cleaners by the mall. They've offered to pay for the new ones but it'll take a week to get them."

"Sheriff in blue jeans," Ed remarked. "Sounds like a magazine cover story. I can see the photos now!"

"Yeah, me too!"

"Bet you're missing Ernie about now."

She shook her head. "You don't know the half of it."

"Me, too," Ed added woefully. "If Ernie was still here, he could've given Joe a place to stay while he tries to get back with Sarah."

"I thought he was staying with you?"

"That's it! He *is* staying with me!"

"Problems?"

"He's messing with my love life, Sheriff. And the darn fool thinks everybody has to be married, even though *his* life is a mess! Between him setting me up with every single woman this side of fifty and moaning about Sarah, I can't take much more."

"You'll work it out."

"I went to see Sarah," he confided. "She won't tell me what happened but she's still mad. She won't even *talk* to him!"

"I'm sure they'll be okay. They've been married forever. Sarah's a wonderful woman."

"That's mostly the problem, I think," Ed told her. "She's too good for Joe. He's miserable and he's making me miserable with him."

"I would think him fixing you up with every woman he knows would be good for you," Sharyn quipped, trying not to laugh.

Ed pulled his little boy face into a frown. "I can get my *own* dates! I don't need Joe finding me women who only want to know if I can remodel my house for them after we get married! I'm happy being single. Or I was until Joe was there all the time! I brought Jessie around for coffee last Saturday night after the show. Joe was waiting up for us with sandwiches! We ate and Jessie left. Joe asked me if I wanted to play cards." He shook his head. "That's not my idea of a good time!"

Sharyn laughed a little, then schooled her mouth into a properly serious frown. "I'm sure it won't last much longer."

"Will you talk to Sarah for me?"

"Don't you mean for *him*?"

He groaned. "At this point, I mean for *me*! I gotta get rid of Joe!"

When they got back to the office, things were quiet. Joe

was out on patrol. JP was doing paperwork. Sharyn imagined that reporters would be interested in the bear attack but it wasn't the same as a murder. Murders were better reading. She prayed that Sam Two Rivers was wrong about the bear attack. She didn't want to think about another murder investigation.

"Mail's here," Trudy called out as they entered the office. She handed Sharyn a stack of mail. "Your mother called and reminded you to call a plumber. And there's someone waiting in your office."

Knowing Nick wouldn't be ready that soon, she approached her office door with serious trepidation. "The mayor?"

"Nope."

"ADA?"

"Nope."

"Do I want to know?"

Trudy broke out into a big smile. "I think you will."

Sharyn nodded uncertainly and took off her jacket. "Okay. Is there any coffee?"

Trudy kept her from going to get it herself by jumping up and running to the coffee maker. "Just go inside, Sheriff!"

Sharyn glanced around the room, noticing that the regular volunteers and JP were staring at her. Whoever was in there had made quite an impression on them. She opened the door to her office.

Ernie got up from the chair in front of her desk. "Sharyn."

"Ernie!" She broke out in a wide smile, almost jumping up and down to get to him and hug him. "I'm so glad to see you!"

Ernie hugged her back and cleared his throat. He realized that he shouldn't have had any doubt about her reception. Sharyn was always Sharyn. "It's good to see you, too."

"Where have you been? You might not be a deputy anymore but you could keep in touch!"

"I know," he admitted, looking at her. "I swear, being sheriff agrees with you! You look great!" He looked down at her jeans in surprise . . . and disapproval.

"Don't ask!" she recommended, walking around to her chair behind her father's big desk. "So, you know what we've been doing. What about you? How's Annie?"

"Well." He shook his head and resumed his seat. "We've done some traveling. Went down to Mexico for a few weeks. Finally saw Disney World. We took Annie's daughter there."

"That's wonderful," Sharyn said, promising herself that she wouldn't bring up the deputy position that she was going to have to fill. She was his friend, too. She didn't want him to feel like he couldn't come and see her without being badgered about being a deputy again. "How's Annie's daughter doing?'

"She and Annie are fine. They're beginning to work on their relationship again. I think they were close to begin with. They'll be close again."

Sharyn nodded. "I know that had to be hard for Annie."

"Oh yeah," Ernie agreed with a nod.

Trudy bustled in with coffee for both of them. "There you are, Ernie! Just the way you like it!"

"Thanks, Trudy! I had some pecan pie last week at Thistle Downs that wasn't even half as good as yours!"

"The country club, huh?" Trudy asked with a smile. "Somebody must be moving up in the world!"

Ernie grinned. "Annie has a membership there."

"Of course," Trudy said smartly. "Just don't wait so long between visits next time!" She nodded to Sharyn, darting her eyes towards Ernie and nodding quickly. Then she walked out, closing the door behind her.

Sharyn knew all that eye and head movement was urging

her to ask Ernie to come back to the department. She sipped her coffee and refused to take the hint.

"So, your mama is gonna marry Senator Talbot, huh?"

"I guess she is."

"She'll be the perfect political wife," Ernie told her. "She always was for your daddy. Talbot will be proud of her. She'll fit right in at the capitol."

"I know." Sharyn sighed. "I just wish I could look at him without wondering what game he's playing!"

"Sharyn," he counseled quietly. "Talbot knew your mama before you were born. He probably really cares for her."

She smiled. "I wish I felt that way."

"Give him a chance. You might."

"When did you get to be such a big fan of Caison Talbot's?" she puzzled.

"He's not so bad." He shrugged. "I'm a big fan of your mama! She deserves to be happy. It wasn't her fault that your daddy died and left her alone."

"I know."

They each drank their coffee in silence. Sharyn glanced up at the portraits of her grandfather, Jacob, and her father, T. Raymond, on the wall. They were both glaring at her, urging her to ask Ernie to come back to the department. She looked resolutely away from them.

"I didn't come here today just for the conversation, Sharyn," Ernie finally confided.

"Is something wrong?" she asked.

He nodded. "I'm miserable, Sharyn. I'd like my job back."

Sharyn almost choked on her coffee. She put her cup down quickly. "Ernie!"

"I know," he began, getting up and pacing the floor. "I know I blew it all. The pension, the rank. I know it's gone. But I'm only forty-eight, Sharyn. I've got another twenty years to give. I wouldn't expect to start back where I was. I know you'll have to put me on a list for the position and that's okay."

"Ernie—"

"Annie and I are on the rocks over this but I don't want to live this way. This department has been a big part of my life for twenty-five years. I can't just give it all up! I don't *want* to give it up!"

Sharyn kept herself from bouncing up out of her chair like a kid and hugging him. She held on to her coffee mug instead and focused on her desk calendar. "What about Annie?"

"I'm a law man. She knew that when we fell in love. She said she understood that it was dangerous and she could live with it." He looked at her. "I want to be with Annie but I don't want to give up my job."

"What will you do if she won't stay with you like that, Ernie?" Sharyn asked carefully. She felt like she was prying into his personal life and she didn't like it. She knew she had no choice. "If you come back and she won't stay with you, you'll have to leave again! We all know that you've never loved anyone else. You waited for her since high school."

Ernie's thin face was set in lines of misery. Sharyn noticed for the first time that he had shaved off the mustache he'd grown after he and Annie had found each other again. "There's only two things I've ever wanted in life, Sharyn. Annie and this job. I've tried living with Annie, without the job and I've been miserable. I've lived without Annie, with the job and I've been miserable. I have to believe we can find a way to work it out so that I can have both. It doesn't seem like that much to ask, does it?"

Sharyn shook her head, not trusting herself to speak.

"Well, I know you'll want to think this over," Ernie said in a gruff voice, his eyes filled with tears that he wiped away with a quick hand. "Just give me a holler when you make your decision, Sharyn. You know I'll respect you, whatever it is."

It took her until he had reached the front door of the sheriff's office before she could say it without making a blubbering fool of herself. "Ernie!" she managed from her office doorway.

He looked back at her with his hand on the heavy door. "Sheriff?"

"Can you report to work in the morning? I think your official leave of absence must be over."

"Sheriff?" he asked hopefully.

"You heard me, Deputy. If you want to get back to work, report in the morning. Six A.M."

Ed whooped loudly from his chair. Trudy started crying and threw herself at Ernie. One of the volunteers walked over and slapped Ernie on the back before he shook his hand. JP came over carefully for an introduction.

"Man, it's gonna be good to have you back!" Ed told him with a wink at Sharyn.

Sharyn closed her office door and leaned against it heavily, relief flooding through her body. Maybe in twenty years she might be able to face Ernie retiring but for now, she was just glad to have him back!

The rest of the day went quickly and easily. Sharyn filled out paperwork explaining why they'd taken the helicopter up the mountain, justifying the expense. She filed her reports to the county commission and the city, in triplicate.

Joe brought in a man who was assaulting a motorist on a side street. JP spoke with the Hispanic construction worker whose truck wouldn't start. The other man had broken out his back window with a hammer. He agreed to press charges against the impatient driver who was still so belligerent that he had to be taken downstairs. Sharyn called the DA's office. It was only about five minutes after Sharyn's request that the DA's office called back.

"Line two," Trudy told her. "Regular as clockwork."

Sharyn resisted the urge to scream. Ever since the last murder investigation, District Attorney Jack Winter had made a habit of requesting Sharyn's presence at his office when she called about an arrest. Technically, it wasn't her job to go to his office and explain details of the case to him. He had simply changed the rules.

She'd tried sending a few others in her place but Jack Winter was adamant that it had to be the sheriff. When she didn't go, things went wrong with the arrest. It was some kind of strange cat-and-mouse game that Winter was playing. After he'd set Lennie Albert up to spy on her, she knew she couldn't trust him. The question was, what was the game?

"I'm on my way to the courthouse, Trudy," she told her assistant as she walked through the office.

"Really?" Trudy muttered. "What a surprise!"

"I know."

"Maybe he likes you, Sheriff," Trudy suggested.

"What?"

"You know." Trudy waggled her eyebrows up and down. "Maybe he *likes* you. That would solve your problem about who to take to your mother's engagement party."

"I don't think he likes me in *any* way. I think this is some weird political maneuvering for him. And are you suggesting I should date Jack Winter?"

Trudy smiled at her. Her brown hair was swept back from her plain face but her brown eyes were shining as she looked at Sharyn. "You know who *I'd* suggest that you should date!"

"Skip it," Sharyn advised. "I don't think I really want to know."

"We all know the two of you were meant for each other!

I declare I don't know why you're both so stubborn! Do him good if Jack Winter *did* ask you out! Maybe that would put a fire in his pants!"

Sharyn laughed and shook her head. "I don't want to know who you're talking about."

Trudy rolled her eyes. "You already know!"

Sharyn walked down the stairs to the street. The cold wind was whipping along the sidewalk. She'd left her coat inside since it was only a short walk to the pink granite courthouse that dwarfed the sheriff's office next door. Workers were building an annex that would connect the sheriff's office to the courthouse and provide more jail space as well as an easy access to take prisoners to court. It would take about a year. Like everything else in Diamond Springs and the surrounding county, growth was coming faster than they could make changes to accommodate it.

Lennie Albert greeted her at the door to the DA's office. His handsome, dark face that he'd been so careful not to scar as a professional football player creased into a wide smile. "Sheriff! Good to see you!"

"Hello, Lennie."

Lennie looked affronted. "You don't sound happy to see me. I'd hate to think there were hard feelings between us."

"No hard feelings," she responded coldly. "I'm just not sure when I talk to you who else I'm talking to!"

"It wasn't that way. Honestly. I admire you, Sheriff. I was only trying to help."

She looked him right in the eye. "Yourself, Lennie. You were only trying to help yourself at everyone else's expense."

He stopped smiling. "I'm sorry you feel that way. The DA is waiting for you inside. I'll just be on my way."

Sharyn stepped into the DA's office. As always, she was overwhelmed by the elegance of Jack Winter's office. It could probably have paid for another helicopter by itself. Somehow, he never had trouble getting funding. Everyone said that Jack Winter had a secret he held about everyone in the Diamond Springs community. Sometimes, she believed the rumors.

"Come in, Sharyn," the DA greeted her. "Let's talk by the fire. You must be freezing."

Sharyn took one of the two chairs by the hearth, across the wide room from the desk.

"Cocoa?" he asked her, standing at the beverage bar that was usually occupied by more potent spirits. "You see? I remember that you don't drink. At least not on duty."

"Sure." She gave in for once, feeling as though she were a log trapped in a fast-moving river. She was slowly being whittled away by the current. "I came for the paperwork on Roger Fox."

"Oh yes," he agreed. "The violent driver."

Sharyn watched him pour the steaming hot chocolate into a small china cup. His suit was impeccable. His shoes always had a shine. His gray hair was always perfectly combed. Jack Winter was as elegant and expensive looking as his office.

He handed her the fragile cup and smiled at her, his bright blue eyes encompassing her face. "How have you been, Sharyn? Things have been quiet for a while."

"I'm fine. And you?"

"Always fine, thank you. I heard about the bear incident this morning." He took the high-backed wing chair opposite her. "That was a messy business."

"Yes, it was."

"Don't tell me you were out there?"

"Of course," she said at once. "I'm the sheriff."

He shook his head. "How unfortunate."

"That I'm the sheriff?" she asked.

"No." His eyes went over her quickly but thoroughly. "I

find that to be very good for both of us, right now. I meant your involvement in the bear death. If I'd known ahead, I would have planned something—"

Sharyn put down her cup. "Like a small seminar?" She thought about the unexpected conference she'd been called to with the governor just after the first bear attack.

Jack Winter smiled. "That would be a good idea. I wish I'd thought of it."

It grated on her nerves that this man might be trying to use his office to manipulate her. "What do you want from these little chats, Mr. Winter?"

"Jack, please." He sipped his coffee. "I want to keep the lines of communication open between our offices."

"So you don't have to send in another spy?" she wondered tautly.

His smile remained intact while he considered her words. "I only want to help you."

Sharyn stood. "You can help me by giving me the paperwork on this arrest."

"It's right out there on my secretary's desk," he explained. "I wasn't trying to keep it from you."

"Thanks for the cocoa."

"I stock it here for you." He stood and faced her. "Sharyn?"

"Yes?"

"I have something I've wanted to ask you."

He put down his coffee cup and then straightened up beside her. They were almost the same height. "I'd like to see you."

"I'm here almost every week."

He smiled. "I meant socially. Perhaps Senator Talbot's engagement party?"

"Oh."

"Does that mean, oh, yes you'd like to. Or oh, I don't

think so. I know I've heard rumors about you and Dr. Thomopolis, but you are still single and—"

"The rumors aren't true," she told him quickly, then realized what she was saying. She was stymied for a moment by not wanting to accept his invitation, yet not wanting to use Nick as her excuse.

"Think about it," he coaxed. He pressed his card into her hand. "Take your time."

He was so close that she could smell his aftershave. She could see the small lines that fanned out from his eyes. Sharyn slid the card into her pocket and walked out of his office without saying another word. She didn't forget to pick up the arrest papers but she didn't slow down or blink her eyes until she heard Joe call her name. She was on the sidewalk between the courthouse and the sheriff's office. The cold wind slapped her in the face.

"Sheriff?" Joe called her again.

"Yes?" She blinked her eyes and looked at him.

"You look like you just saw a ghost!"

"Not a ghost." She glanced at the courthouse behind her. "Maybe a demon. What are you doing out here?"

"Just came back from lunch at the diner. What's up between you and Winter anyway? Are you seeing him?"

"Only when I have to."

Joe shrugged his broad, straight shoulders. He was a tough-looking man in his late forties. He'd been a deputy with the department since Sharyn went off to college. "I have a friend. I know you need a date to go to your mother's engagement party. He's a nice guy. A fireman. He's been married once but—"

Sharyn glared at him. "Why is everyone so worried about me having a date to the engagement party?"

"Because we know you're single and we know you don't want to go alone." He smiled at her. "Anyway, this friend of mine, Ham—"

"Ham?"

"Short for Hamilton. He's a great guy. You'll like him."

"I don't need help finding a date."

He smiled at her like an older brother. "Well, we all know you don't exactly *need* help. Just a little nudge in the right direction."

"Joe!"

"But you're too stubborn to admit it!"

"What about you and Sarah?" Sharyn couldn't see Joe's dark eyes behind the mirrored sunglasses he always wore but his whole attitude changed when she mentioned Sarah's name.

He ran his hand through his short, spiked, dark hair and shook his head. "I don't know what to say about me and Sarah."

"What happened? Why did she kick you out?"

"She didn't kick me out," Joe answered slowly. "She asked me to leave. She said I don't understand her anymore. After twenty years of marriage and three kids!"

"Something must have brought it on," Sharyn prompted. If he could pry into her personal life, she decided, she could pry into his. Besides, it was for the good of the department. If Ed got any more upset about his own personal life, she could lose two deputies.

"It was stupid," Joe confessed. "It was dinner out and a show. I stayed late at the firing range. We missed our reservation. Sarah said I always do things like that because I don't like to go out."

"Do you?"

"No!" He adjusted his neck. "I'm not crazy about going out but I go along with it. I just lost track of time."

Sharyn guessed it was more than just that one dinner and a show but that was as far as she was willing to go. Joe tended to be more interested in his weeks out with the Reserve than he was in social activities with his wife. Sarah was probably unhappy about it. But they had been together for a long time. She knew they would find a way to compromise.

David Matthews, another deputy and Joe's nephew, passed them on his way into the office. He didn't see them.

"He didn't look too happy." Sharyn hurried up the stairs to the office.

"He was driving his own car, too, instead of one of those fine machines the Widow Richmond lets him drive," Joe observed. "Something must be up there, too."

Sharyn shook her head. "That was a strange relationship anyway. Maybe she just unattached herself to him the way she attached herself during the murder investigation." Beau Richmond's wife had started dating her deputy the day after she and David went to question her about her husband's murder. It was a very short mourning period.

"Now, they got this bear attack! That family is jinxed!" Joe declared.

"I wonder if this will affect the brother's case against the will?"

"I doubt it," Joe said, holding the door for her. "I'm sure he'll still want that money! He can always buy himself another wife with it!"

"Your mother called again about the plumber, Sheriff," Trudy told her as she walked into the warm office from the cold outside. "And there's a woman that's been on hold waiting for you to get back. She says she's Darva Richmond's aunt and she has to talk to you."

"Thanks, Trudy," she said, taking the messages from her.

"JP's waiting to talk to you, too."

Sharyn looked up at her new deputy. "JP?"

The deputy shrugged. "I only waited to tell you that I was going home. This was my last split shift. Unless you need me to do more."

"No." Sharyn smiled and patted his arm. "You've done

fine! You can plan on starting to work the night shift day after tomorrow. Take tomorrow off. The next night you'll come in around this time and work with David. Okay?"

"Yes!" He smiled. "Thank you, Sheriff Howard."

"Thank you, JP. You're going to be a great asset to this department."

JP blushed and nodded his head, glancing around himself at Trudy's smiling face and Joe's accepting one. "Thank you. I will work hard for you, Sheriff Howard."

"I know you will," she answered. "Say hello to Benita and the kids for me."

"I will." He smiled again, then left the station.

"What was that all about?" David asked.

"Joe can fill you in," Trudy put him off. "Sheriff, line one for that caller."

Sharyn nodded. "Thanks, Trudy." She went into her office and rubbed her cold hands together before she picked up the phone. "This is Sheriff Howard."

"A lady sheriff?" the woman's voice asked on the other end of the line.

"That's right, ma'am. What can I do for you?"

"I'm Eleanore Lacey, Darva Richmond's aunt. I just received word of my niece's death."

"I'm sorry for your loss, ma'am. I only met your niece once but she seemed to be a very well-liked woman here in Diamond Springs."

"Thank you, Sheriff. What about her death?"

"Ma'am?"

"Do you think there could be foul play?"

"Not really, ma'am." Sharyn played with the pen on her desk. "She was attacked by a bear. It's true that her husband didn't hear the attack but I'm sure he did the best he could in the situation. There wasn't anything I'd call foul play."

"I'm flying down there tonight, Sheriff. There are some things you should know."

"Do you have anything conclusive, ma'am? Any proof there might have been foul play?"

"I don't know. Do you know how soon will my niece be buried?"

"Well, I suppose that will be up to her husband, Ms. Lacey. We don't make those arrangements here."

"Of course, Sheriff. Sorry. What about the autopsy?"

"We aren't going to do an autopsy, Ms. Lacey. Unless you do have something more than just a feeling about your niece's death."

"Please don't release her body to him until I get there," the old woman pleaded. "I don't want anything covered up."

"Ma'am," Sharyn added, trying to make the woman understand. "There wouldn't be much to cover up. She was mauled by a bear."

"Just don't do anything until I get there. Please, Sheriff!"

"Yes, ma'am," Sharyn agreed. What could it hurt?

"I'll be arriving there later tonight but I'll be in your office first thing tomorrow morning!"

"Yes, ma'am."

"A lady sheriff! Belle Starr would've been proud!"

"I suppose so," Sharyn said with a smile.

"Until tomorrow, Sheriff Howard."

"Goodbye, ma'am." Sharyn hung up the phone thoughtfully. She didn't want to think that Darva Richmond's death was anything but a tragic accident. Without some substantial evidence to the contrary, it would have to remain an accident. On the other hand, she didn't want to discount the possibility that it could be more than it seemed. Just because she didn't want to go through another murder investigation so soon didn't mean she could turn a blind eye to the facts. If there were any facts.

There was a knock on her door. David poked his head into the room. "Sheriff, can I talk to you?"

"Sure, David. What's up?"

David slumped down in the chair opposite her. "It's Julia. We broke up over the weekend."

"I'm sorry, David."

"I think it's the stress of this whole thing with her family. I mean, when Beau was killed, they all moved into the mansion with her. Then Beau's brother and his wife came down to contest the will. The tension is awful."

"I'm sure it must be hard."

"I think maybe if I could get her out of there, it could help."

"Maybe."

"What would you do?"

Sharyn glanced up at him. "What would I . . . I don't know."

"Well, you're a woman." He looked at her significantly. "Would you want to be taken away if you were in her position?"

"Maybe."

"Would you want it to be a surprise?"

"I'm not much on surprises," she said.

"I'm thinking I could go and pick her up and take her to my place."

"Just be careful she doesn't see it as kidnapping."

David laughed. "I think it could work. Thanks, Sheriff."

"Any time, David. JP will be starting to work with you the day after tomorrow. I know you can use the help at night."

"It has been a lot busier the last few months. Who would've thought when we graduated that all of this would happen?"

Sharyn and David had been in the same graduating class

at Diamond Springs High School. "Not me," she answered truthfully.

"Me either. Life's strange, sometimes. Like that bear attack today."

"I know."

"Well, I'm going out on patrol. I think that's gonna work with Julia. I think it's just stress."

"I hope it helps, David. It'll be a big change for her going from the mansion with servants and everything, to your apartment."

"Yeah. She'll have to learn to cook."

Sharyn thought that was unlikely but she kept it to herself. Since there were no emergencies and nothing pressing, she was getting ready to leave for home at six. She had already closed up her backpack and put on her jacket when she looked up to see Nick standing at her office door. "Oh no."

Nick leaned up against the doorframe. "Now why is it that I have that effect on you?"

Sharyn buttoned up her jacket. "Because I'm the sheriff and I know that look on your face."

He smiled. "Got any dinner plans?"

She groaned. "Now I know it's bad news."

"What? I always ask you out to dinner when I have something bad to say?"

"Pretty much."

"Well, how about dinner?"

Sharyn thought about the rumors. She thought about Jack Winter. She picked up her backpack. "Okay. Let's go."

Chapter Three

Nick had his black Cadillac parked out by the curb so they took his car. Sharyn's Jeep was in the police parking lot in back.

Joe nodded his head. Ed grinned and winked at her. Trudy smiled and waved as they left together. She managed to get in a little something about Jack Winter monopolizing Sharyn's time.

"Is that true?" Nick asked her when they got into his car.

"Jack Winter is the DA," Sharyn reminded him. "He has the right to ask me about criminal cases."

"That's not the way Trudy sounded," he retorted, pulling the car out into traffic. "What did she mean about him being interested in you?"

"Nick, did you come by the office to discuss my personal life or did you have something professional you wanted to tell me?"

He glanced at her. "You're prickly tonight."

Sharyn sighed and looked out of the window. "Where are we going?"

"Antonio's. It's a new place by the mall."

"Don't mention the mall," she requested. She told him about her uniforms.

"I was wondering why you were wearing jeans today. I thought it was a new look for you. Country sheriff kind of thing."

"I'm surprised the commission didn't want to see me about something today so they could ask me about it."

"What color did they dye the uniforms?"

"Blue."

He laughed. "Maybe you could petition the commission to let you wear jeans all the time instead of the uniform. You look good in jeans."

Sharyn glanced at him carefully, looking away when he looked back at her. "Thanks."

"You're welcome. So, what's up with Winter?" he asked, thinking that she might be ready to talk about it.

"Nothing. He just—" She paused, then shook her head. "He asked me out."

"*What?*"

"Is that so hard to believe? Just because I'm the sheriff doesn't mean I can't date!"

Nick ground his teeth in frustration. "Winter must be thirty years older than you!"

"And? Does that mean he doesn't date?"

Nick brought his car to an abrupt halt in front of Antonio's. "Are you telling me that you're in love with Jack Winter?"

"I'm not in love with Jack Winter!"

"Are you going to see him?"

"Probably every time there's an arrest!"

"I mean *personally,*" he replied, turning to face her in the warm interior of the car. "Are you going to go out *personally* with Jack Winter?"

"No! The man makes my skin crawl!"

They were almost face-to-face. The red Antonio's Villa light was glaring into the car. Nick swallowed hard. Sharyn took a deep, ragged breath.

"All right."

"Are we arguing about whether or not I'm going to date Jack Winter?"

Nick straightened his tie. "I think so."

"Is there some reason that it makes a difference to you?"

"I . . . care about what happens to you, you know. Winter is a dangerous man. He's not someone you want to mess around with." He looked at her, then opened his car door. "Are we going to eat or what?"

Antonio's was large but intimate, with candlelit tables and soft music playing in the background. Sharyn hadn't eaten there before. She was surprised that Nick brought her there.

"It's dark in here," she said as they were seated.

"Perfect for some wine," the waiter suggested. "And for the gentleman to see the young woman at her best, eh?"

"We work together," Sharyn snarled. "That's it!"

"Of course," the waiter said, leaving their menus.

"You didn't have to bite his head off," Nick admonished.

"Someone has to put a stop to the rumors about you and me."

"Rumors? About you and me?"

"Don't tell me no one said anything to you? Even Jack Winter—" She bit her tongue.

". . . thinks there's something going on between you and me?" he wondered, a smile spreading across his face. Then he frowned. "But he thought he'd ask you out anyway?"

She shrugged. "I'm starving." She changed the subject, sorry she'd brought it up. She just didn't want him to think *she* was behind the rumors. "I wonder what's good?"

Ten minutes later, they had ordered their meals and had a glass of wine in front of each of them. Sharyn glanced

across the table at Nick in the warm glow of the candlelight.

Nick was ten years older than she. He'd come to Diamond Springs the year she had graduated from high school.
Her father had thought the world of him but the first two
years after she'd become sheriff, he'd been impossible. He
didn't seem quite so impossible in the last months. She
didn't know if he was growing on her or if he had changed
towards her. Either way, he'd been indispensable in the last
murder case. They weren't exactly friends but they certainly weren't adversaries anymore. The idea that they were
something more brought a rosy blush to her cheeks, even
though she knew that it was ridiculous.

"So, what did you find that's going to make my life
miserable?"

He laughed. "Honey. I knew you wouldn't like it."

Sharyn choked on her wine, covering her mouth with her
linen napkin. "Wh-what did you say?"

"Honey? Are you okay?"

"Are you—are you calling me *honey*?"

Nick smiled slowly. "I wouldn't call you honey, even if
this *wasn't* a business dinner."

Sharyn considered his words. "Why?"

He shrugged. "Not my choice of endearments. Sweetheart, maybe."

"Oh." She drank some of her wine. It was very warm in
the restaurant. Probably all the candles, she decided.

He leaned across the table towards her. "What about
you?"

"Me?" she asked in a squeaky voice.

"Your choice of endearments. What would you call the
love of your life?"

She looked at his hand. It was on the table just a fraction
of an inch from hers on the white tablecloth. She moved
her finger experimentally. It would take only the smallest

gesture to touch him. For an instant, she wondered what he would say if she put her hand on his and smiled at him.

Nick sat back in his chair as Sharyn jumped up from the table. One second, he was looking into her big, blue eyes and the next, she was on her feet.

"I have to go!"

"We haven't eaten!"

"To the ladies' room! I have to go to the ladies' room!"

Nick swallowed the rest of his wine as she all but ran out of the dining room. He didn't know what he'd said or done but it appeared that he'd blown it again. He saw a small piece of paper flutter out of her jeans pocket as she left him. He picked it up from the burgundy carpet and looked at it. It was Jack Winter's card. With deliberate malice, he ripped it in half and put it under his napkin.

Sharyn returned as the food was arriving. She was in control again. She kept her hands near her plate or in her lap. "So, what are you trying to tell me?"

For just an instant, Nick thought about blurting it out. He was willing to take the chance that she might not feel the same and that they wouldn't be able to work together after he was done. Then he shook his head and did a quick reality check. "There was honey on the body. The clear stuff you saw? It was honey."

"Honey?"

"It was smeared all over her. I'd like to do more work on her. I thought this might be enough to warrant an autopsy. Unless the bear brought along her own condiments, the chances are that Darva Richmond didn't drizzle herself with the stuff."

"There isn't a chance that she . . . that they . . . she and Donald."

He shook his head, getting the idea. "I don't think so. It was in her hair and all over her clothes."

"So, what are you thinking?"

"I don't know," he admitted. "I just think it warrants a second look and an autopsy."

"It would go along with a phone call I had from her aunt today."

"Oh?"

"She said that she felt Darva's death might be foul play."

"That's interesting. Did she say why she thought that?"

"Not exactly," Sharyn replied. "She's supposed to get here tonight and explain tomorrow."

"Autopsy?"

"I think so."

"Do we have to ask the county first?"

"No. If we both authorize the death as being suspicious, we're fine. We'll worry about it later if nothing else turns up."

He looked satisfied with her decision. "You're a good sheriff, Sharyn."

"Because I agreed with you?"

He let it go. "No. I was just thinking that you work hard and you do a good job. You don't let anything interfere with what you think is right, even if it means you might not be sheriff again."

Sharyn drank the last of her wine and shook her head when the waiter offered more. "Coffee, please?" She glanced at Nick as she put some pasta on her fork. "So you think I won't be re-elected?"

"I didn't say that," he answered. "But I do think things have changed and voters sometimes blame the wrong people for those changes. What would you do if you weren't re-elected?"

She shrugged. "I don't know. It happened so fast that I was elected in the first place, I haven't had time to think about anything but the job. I'm done with law school. All I'd have to do is pass the bar and I could be a lawyer."

"That would be interesting," he conceded. "You could

lose the election and represent some of the people you arrested."

Sharyn laughed. "I don't think that would be ethical. Besides, I don't intend to lose the election."

"So, you envision yourself being sheriff forever?" He studied her face in the candlelight. "Have you thought about how your—er—potential husband could feel about that?"

"I don't have a potential husband. But if I did, he'd have to understand what it means to me," she answered quietly. "Not that I have any plans to be married or re-elected."

Nick smiled. "You could meet the right man and he could change your whole perspective."

Sharyn sat back in her chair as the waiter took her plate. "I can't imagine a man who would fall in love with a sheriff who can't cook, isn't all that good with household stuff, and usually manages to spill something when she's around liquids. Add my hours on the job to that and I don't see anyone coming along to sweep me off my feet." She smiled at him. "Now, can we talk about your personal life."

"What's to say?" he asked defensively. "I take apart dead bodies for a living. That's real special to women."

"I've seen you date," she responded. "Women find you . . . attractive."

He laughed. "You haven't been to my house. Once a woman sees it, they mark me off as marriage material."

"I've seen your office," she agreed. "That was bad enough!"

"I never thought about getting married until—"

"Until?"

"Until . . . the last few years. I'm getting old, I guess. When you get to be my age, you start thinking about wanting someone to take care of you, someone you can take care of."

"I don't think that has anything to do with age," she

quipped. "Everyone thinks about wanting someone to take care of them."

"Do you?" he wondered. "You always seem too independent for that kind of thing."

"I'm human," she answered. "I've thought about it a lot lately. I guess because my mother is going to marry the senator."

"Speaking of that," Nick began carefully, not wanting to break their rapport, "I got an invitation to the engagement party."

"So did I."

"Are you going to go?"

Sharyn sighed. "I don't have much choice. My mother already thinks I hate Caison and I want to ruin her wedding."

Nick took a deep breath. "Well, if you're going to go and I'm going to go, we could go—"

Sharyn's cell phone went off. Her heart was already pounding. The sudden sound made her jump. "Sorry. Just a minute." She answered the phone. It was Foster Odom from the newspaper again. She spoke quickly to him, then closed the phone. "That man is driving me crazy!"

"Who was it?" Nick wondered. Whoever it was, he wanted to strangle him.

"Foster Odom, the new reporter at the *Gazette*."

"Is he already on this foul play angle?"

"No," Sharyn said. "He's into calling this a rabid bear attack."

"That might be worse."

"I know."

Nick started to take out his credit card and give it to the waiter.

"Let me get my half of that," Sharyn said quickly.

"I asked you to dinner," he told her bluntly, giving his card to the waiter. "I'll pay."

"Well, I guess it's a tax deduction," she replied lamely.

Nick leaned forward intently. "Sharyn, I—"

Sharyn's phone rang again. "I'm sorry, Nick. Just a minute." It was Bruce Bellows with the wildlife agency. Sharyn spoke with him quickly, then closed the phone. "I have to go. Bruce Bellows says a group of hunters are on the mountain. They plan on killing all the bears to get to the rabid ones."

Nick didn't let his disappointment show. "I'll drive you. We'll get there faster from here."

"Thanks."

Diamond Mountain was alive with lights, howling dogs, and hunters when they arrived at the top. Reporters were busy setting up their equipment. Caution signs that Bruce had put out to close off the road had been knocked down and trampled under the big wheels of trucks and sport utility vehicles. The wildlife manager was standing with Sam Two Rivers at the closed gate into the park. They were facing the angry, armed mob of men and women without any weapons of their own.

"I have a gun," Nick volunteered as he swung the Cadillac in between several large trucks.

"I know," she answered. "Several of them. But we're not going to shoot anyone tonight so you might as well leave it here."

Nick looked at the group of hunters in their camouflage clothes and painted faces. "I feel like I'm in Lord of the Flies! Are you sure you want to go out there without a gun?"

She appreciated his anxiety. "Maybe you should stay here."

"I'm an emergency deputy!"

"All right." She took a deep breath. "Come on then, Deputy. No guns!"

Sharyn walked through the crowd and reached Bruce

Bellow's side with Nick following close behind her. The four of them stood in front of the fifty or so hunters.

"Don't try to stop us, Sheriff!"

"You know that's why I'm here, John," she answered the man. "This is a state sanctuary. Hunting is illegal."

"There's rabid bears up here killing people!"

"There aren't any rabid bears, Dan! That was just a story in the paper!"

"Two people been killed up here, Sheriff! We're not going home until we take care of the problem!"

"You're about to become the problem, Zeke," Sharyn replied. "We all live here. We all know each other. This is trespassing on state land. If you don't leave now, I'll have to arrest all of you and that new jail's not finished yet. It'll be a tight squeeze!"

A few people laughed but a few weren't so easily amused.

"It's our home and our lives, Sheriff! If the bears are rabid, we deserve to know!"

"And if the bears were rabid, Steve, I'd be up here telling you that! There are no rabid bears! In fact," she glanced at Nick, "we're going to be investigating the last killing up here as a suspicious death."

That broke up the focus of the crowd.

"A murder? Are you saying the woman was murdered?"

"I don't know for sure what happened yet," she answered truthfully. "But there are some questions that don't involve the bear. Go home. We'll let you know what develops!"

The crowd was starting to talk among themselves. Guns were lowered and some of the hunters started back for their trucks. A few lingered, unsatisfied, talking to the press.

"Thanks, Sheriff," Bruce said in a relieved whisper. "I guess I should call for some reinforcements from the state. I won't let them kill off the bears because of this incident."

"Hold off on that call for now, Bruce," Sharyn persuaded. "They'll wait to see what happens. And I'm going to ring that scrawny reporter's neck who printed that story!"

Bruce laughed. "Made me wish I carried a gun there for a while!"

"Now you know how my people have felt for generations," Sam said with a grim smile. "Sheriff Howard, you can stand in front of a mob at my side any time."

"Thanks, Sam." She laughed. "Excuse me if I don't take you up on that offer any time soon!"

When the crowd had dispersed, Nick drove Sharyn back to the office for her Jeep. "That went better than I thought it would," he admitted.

"Even without a gun," she added.

"Yeah. Although I would've felt better *with* a gun!"

"They can make things worse sometimes."

He nodded. "That was the way your father was."

"I know. That might have been what killed him."

Nick frowned. "I don't think so. There was no way he could've known—"

She smiled sadly. "I know."

"He was a good man and a good sheriff."

"He was, wasn't he?"

Nick put his hand over hers on the car seat between them. "His daughter is a good woman and a good sheriff."

Sharyn felt like a boulder was lodged in her throat. "Thanks."

"And I'd like to take you—"

"Sheriff?" Charlie, the impound lot supervisor, knocked on the window. "Sheriff Howard? You leaving anytime soon?" The old man peered in through the window, trying to see them. "Hello? Nick? Is that you?"

"Hi Charlie!" Nick rolled down his window. "I'll talk to you tomorrow, Sharyn. I'll let you know if I find anything."

"Thanks, Nick," she said, her whole body feeling overheated. "I'll see you tomorrow. Thanks for dinner. I think I must owe you a meal."

"I think so," he retorted. "Next time, you can take me out."

Sharyn laughed, relieved to get out of the car. The rumor mill would get enough gossip because they ate dinner together at Antonio's.

"Bad situation, huh, Sheriff?" Charlie asked as she walked to her Jeep with her keys in her hand.

"Uh—yeah, I think so," she stammered, not sure which situation he was referring to.

"Those bears probably didn't mean to hurt anyone," Charlie continued.

"No, they probably didn't. We'll figure it all out."

Charlie laughed. "Know you will, Sheriff! Good night!"

"Good night, Charlie!"

Sharyn drove home, recalling as she turned into the drive that she hadn't called a plumber. Her mother was already in bed asleep as she tiptoed into the house. In the morning, she would call the plumber, she promised herself and her mother. First thing in the morning.

First thing in the morning came twenty minutes late. Sharyn forgot to set her alarm clock. Half awake and wet from her shower in cold water because her mother had just used up all the hot water, she was searching for her uniforms when she remembered that she didn't have any. She hopped into a pair of jeans and a white button-down shirt. She ran a comb through her copper curls, then put on her badge and gun.

"Aren't you going to eat breakfast?" Faye Howard asked as her daughter ran by, putting on her jacket.

"Not this morning," she answered. "See you later."

Her phone was quiet on the way to work. There was a message telling her that her number had been changed. So much for Foster Odom calling all the time, she thought, pulling the Jeep into the office parking lot.

Ernie, in uniform, met her at the door, his clipboard in hand. "Morning, Sheriff. Eleanore Lacey has been waiting on you for the last half hour. I've got her in the interrogation room. She's a nice old thing. Pretty broken up about her niece. Nick has started the autopsy on Mrs. Richmond. He should know something later today. David had to go out to the Richmond place last night after the bear thing on the mountain. He picked up Donald Richmond for drunk and disorderly after Julia and her family said he'd been going crazy up there."

"We didn't file charges though?" she guessed.

"Not with all he's been through. Just held on to him for his own good."

"Okay."

"Ed's out talking to some of their friends, trying to get a picture of the couple to see if there were any real problems between them."

Sharyn felt as though she'd gone through a time warp. Walking beside Ernie as he filled her in on what was going on was like taking a giant step backwards. Suddenly, everything was all right again. Ernie was back. She was actually smiling by the time she reached her office.

"And I persuaded the company that furnishes the department's uniforms to Fed Ex a couple of new uniforms to you this morning."

She walked into her office and the ugly, brown uniforms were there, hanging on her wall, encased in plastic wrap. She was actually glad to see them. "Oh, Ernie!" She hugged him tightly. "Thanks for being here!"

He adjusted his glasses and turned red. "Ma'am?"

"If you start calling me ma'am again after I've been Sharyn while you haven't been a deputy, I'll fire you on the spot."

Ernie adjusted his glasses a final time, then smiled at her. "Do what you have to do, ma'am."

"Ernie! You know I won't fire you when I'm so happy you're back!"

"My mama always said, don't threaten what you can't back up."

"Fine." Sharyn picked up one of her uniforms. "I can live with it if that's what it takes to have you back. How did Annie take the news?"

"Not well, I'm afraid."

"I'm sorry. Are you—"

"I'm not dead yet, Sheriff. I waited a long time for that lady. I won't let this break us up."

Impulsively, she hugged him again. "I'm going to go and change. I've missed you so much!"

"Even when Lennie was here?"

"Even when Lennie was here."

"You know, folks thought the two of you might end up together."

"Folks need to quit speculating on my life."

He shrugged his thin shoulders. "They won't. You're a public figure. A pretty, single girl at that. They're gonna be watching and waiting to pounce on whatever you do."

"Pretty?"

"Like going out to dinner with Nick last night at Antonio's," he continued. "They were talking about it on the radio this morning. Said you were holding hands."

"We were not! It was a business dinner!"

"People don't care about that," he cautioned. "They only care about the juicy stuff."

"I'm going to change. Then I'll talk to Eleanore Lacey."

He nodded. "I'll just sit in on that and take notes."

"Thanks."

Ernie looked around the office and smoothed his hand

across the big oak desk when Sharyn left. He took a deep breath. It was good to be back.

Eleanore Lacey was a handsome woman, probably in her late sixties or early seventies. Sharyn noticed the family resemblance immediately. The older woman kept her seat when Sharyn and Ernie came into the room, her gloved hand on a heavy cane. She wore a heavy rose perfume that assaulted Sharyn's senses. She sneezed a few times after she walked into the room.

"I'm sorry, Mrs. Lacey," she explained. "Allergies. I'm allergic to roses. Sorry too, that you had to wait so long for me. I hope you had a good flight."

The other woman broke down in tears. "I can't believe Darva is dead!"

Sharyn took her seat across the table from the woman. Ernie handed them both tissues when Sharyn kept sniffling. "As I tried to explain to you on the phone, ma'am, your niece was knocked down and attacked by a bear. We found her, partially eaten, on the mountain. We had no reason to suspect foul play at that time."

Eleanore Lacey leaned slightly towards Sharyn. Her brown eyes were keen in her withered face. "But you do now, don't you?"

"The medical examiner and I have requested an autopsy on the body. There was something questionable found that we felt needed further exploration."

"What was it, Sheriff?"

"I'm not able to say right now, ma'am," Sharyn answered formally. "I can only say that I'll keep you informed. Do you plan to stay for the funeral?"

"Of course." The woman dabbed at her eyes. "And to assist you, Sheriff!"

"Thank you, ma'am."

Ernie helped the old lady to her feet. Her legs were encased in heavy brown wraps. She could barely walk, relying heavily on her cane for support.

"I'd be happy to call a taxi for you, ma'am," Ernie told the woman.

"I would appreciate that, Deputy. I'm staying at your Regency Hotel." She laid her gloved hand on Ernie's. "Please, help my niece. Don't let her killer escape."

Ernie patted her hand. "We'll do the best we can, Mrs. Lacey."

"It's Miss," she assured him with a small smile. "Miss Eleanore."

"We'll do what we can, Miss Eleanore. If your niece was killed, the sheriff won't let whoever did it get away with it."

"Thank you, Deputy—" She looked at his badge. "—Watkins. My niece and I were very close. She was such a beautiful girl."

Ernie helped the old woman down the office stairs and out to the waiting taxi. Sharyn watched them go.

"I wonder why she's so sure something happened besides the bear attack?" she asked when he came back inside.

"She didn't give me any particulars. Maybe it's just a feeling. Maybe Miz Richmond and her husband were having trouble. If Nick's right and that was honey smeared all over his wife, maybe that was what attracted the bear," Ernie suggested.

"Let's have a few words with Donald Richmond before we let him go, huh? We've already got him here, we might as well ask him a few questions."

"I'll have him brought up here," Ernie said.

"Jack Winter called again for you this morning," Trudy told her. "He's like a bee around a flower."

"Are you sure you're not the one who starts these rumors, Trudy?" she asked, looking through her mail.

"And he sent these," Trudy continued, taking out a dozen

paper-covered roses from behind her desk. Her eyes were gleaming brightly. "Any reply?"

Sharyn recoiled from the roses in something like horror. "Maybe you could put them in a vase and set them out here for the whole office to enjoy?"

Trudy laughed. "I sure could, Sheriff! Would you like the card?"

Sharyn took the card and went back into the interrogation room that doubled as their conference room. She took the card out of its envelope and read the message.

> *Sharyn,*
> *I hope you're considering my idea. We would make a*
> *perfect couple!*
> *Jack*

She put the card back in its envelope and put it into her pocket. She'd lost his business card sometime during the excitement last night. Not that he was hard to get in touch with if she wanted to call him.

Ernie came in, escorting Donald Richmond. He looked hung over. His face was pale and his eyes were a little glazed. His clothes were torn and stained and his knuckles were grazed. He smelled like stale whiskey.

"Mr. Richmond?" Sharyn started as Ernie closed the door. "I hope you're feeling better this morning?"

"Better? This is a nightmare! I don't know what to do."

"I'm sorry for your loss, Mr. Richmond."

"You don't understand, Sheriff," he said quickly. "No one understands now that Darva's gone."

Sharyn glanced at Ernie. "Why don't you explain it to us."

Donald Richmond looked around himself wildly. "Am I being charged with something? Can I go?"

Sharyn sat back in her chair and studied the man. He

looked like someone at the end of his rope. He *had* just lost his wife. Even if he had nothing to do with the act, it had to be a terrible thing to see her half eaten and know that he had slept through the attack. "We aren't going to press charges against you for drunk and disorderly, Mr. Richmond. Would you mind if we ask you a few questions?"

Donald glanced at her, then at Ernie. "What about?"

"Your wife and what happened up on the mountain," Sharyn replied.

He shook his head. "Don't I need a lawyer?"

"You aren't being charged with anything," she answered truthfully. "But if you'd feel more comfortable—"

"No," he decided. "I don't care. I don't have anything to hide."

Ernie nodded and took out his notebook.

"What made you and your wife decide to go camping? It's been pretty cold."

"Have you been to the mansion?" Donald laughed. "*That's* cold! Julia and those others. We just couldn't take it another night. We thought we could get away. Not far away because of the problem with the will, but just away together, alone for the night."

"Why not a hotel?"

"I don't know. It sounded romantic to Darva. We met camping in Montana at a national park. The camper belongs to Julia. We didn't know the toilet didn't work until Darva got up during the night. Even so, no one else was up there. We didn't think about bears attacking her."

Sharyn nodded. "Just one last question, Mr. Richmond. Were you and your wife having any problems? I know staying at the mansion is stressful. Was it causing problems between you?"

Donald stared at her. "I know what you're saying, Sheriff! I loved Darva! I didn't kill her!"

Chapter Four

"Slow down, Mr. Richmond," Ernie reassured him. "We aren't accusing you of killing your wife."

"Weren't you?"

"Why would we do that when a bear was responsible?" Sharyn asked.

Donald shook his head. "I don't know. Everything is wrong now. Forget the will. I—I can't do this without Darva!"

"No one is accusing you of anything, Mr. Richmond," Sharyn stated clearly. "I should tell you that we're doing an autopsy on Mrs. Richmond's body. After that, she'll be released to you for burial. I know you don't want to do anything until she's been properly looked after, do you?"

Donald shook his head, too overcome with emotion to speak.

"I'll find somebody to run you home, Mr. Richmond," Ernie said, patting the other man's arm. "You go home and get some sleep. It's hard to lose someone you love."

"Thank you," Donald said, tears slipping down his face.

"I am sorry for your loss, Mr. Richmond," Sharyn said quietly.

Donald Richmond nodded and Ernie took him from the room. Sharyn walked back to her office, thinking about the man. She had doubts about whether she should have held him. They really didn't know yet that Darva's death was a murder. It *was* suspicious. But until she had something more conclusive, she was going to let him go.

"Your mother called, Sheriff," Trudy sang out. "Don't forget the plumber."

"Thanks, Trudy."

Ernie joined her in her office when Donald Richmond was in a squad car on his way back to the mansion. "Well?"

The plumber's line was busy. She hung up the phone. "I don't know, Ernie. He doesn't seem like a killer to me."

"Me, either," he admitted. "He just saw his wife, half eaten by a bear. I can't imagine that happening to Annie. What would it be like?"

The closest thing Sharyn could envision to that was walking into the corner store and seeing her father lying dead on the floor. She shuddered. "I think he acts like a man who's grief stricken. A man who loved his wife. He hasn't tried to run. Just got drunk and made a mess of himself."

Ed knocked on the door and poked his head around. "Ernie! Man, it's great to see you back! How's Annie?"

"She's good," Ernie said, shaking Ed's hand. "It's good to be back."

Ed looked at Sharyn. "Private conference or can anyone join in?"

"We're talking about Donald Richmond."

"You got my agenda then." Ed took a seat beside Ernie. "From what I could find out from their friends, they were the perfect couple. Never a cross word. Always acted like

they were in love. You know. None of them can believe
anything like this could happen to them."

"So, they were happy together?"

"Well, the family is something different," Ed recounted.
"Of course, they don't want Donald there so I took what
they said with a grain of salt."

"What *did* they say?" Ernie wondered.

"Just the opposite of the friends. Always fighting. Bitter
words between them. They didn't sleep together. But the
air in that place is tense, let me tell you! It almost gave me
stomach cramps being there!"

"What about this lawsuit contesting the will?" Sharyn
questioned.

"I checked court docs on that last night," Ernie chipped
in. "It seems that Donald is contesting the will because it
was changed in the last few months of Beau Richmond's
life. As we all know, the widow testified that Beau wasn't
in his right mind during those last few months of his life.
Donald is claiming that he wasn't stable enough to make
out a new will that changed his heir from being his brother
to being his new wife."

Sharyn didn't want to linger around the memories of the
murder case that had rocked the small town and taken Ernie
from her. "Makes sense to me."

"I could see that, too," Ed agreed. "And with Donald
living right there, with all of Julia's relatives who want her
to keep what she has, I can see where that would cause
some serious strain."

Ernie shook his head. "It would make more sense to find
Donald dead. The lawsuit over the will won't stop because
Mrs. Richmond is dead."

"I don't know," Sharyn said, leaning back in her chair.
"Donald just said he might give up on it. Maybe they knew
that about him. Maybe Darva was the push behind the lawsuit. She had everything to gain from Donald inheriting."

Ed frowned. "Take your choice of suspects then, if you decide to go with this being a murder case, Sheriff! Julia, her parents, her Aunt Margaret. Some cousins I didn't know. They all live at the mansion now."

"If we decide to pursue this, let's talk to David. He's spent a lot of time over there. He might have something more definite about one of the family members and Darva Richmond."

"What about the husband?" Ed asked. "Didn't David pick him up for drunk and disorderly last night?"

There was another knock on the door. Nick opened it a crack and glanced inside. "Conference?"

"Come on in, Nick," Sharyn told him. "What are you doing here? I know you can't have anything yet!"

"Actually, I cheated." He stepped into the room, carrying a crystal vase full of long-stem red roses.

Ed grinned and winked at Sharyn. Ernie sat back, smiled and nodded.

Sharyn felt her face turn as red as the roses. She closed her mouth and tried to find her voice. "Uh—are—are those for me?"

Nick looked at the roses and then at Ed and Ernie. He turned to Sharyn. "Yes. I mean, no, not from *me*. Trudy gave them to me when I walked in and told me to bring them in here. Who *are* they from?"

Ed shook his head. Ernie sighed heavily. They looked at each other, then looked away.

Sharyn was on her feet in an instant. "Trudy was supposed to put those out here." She grabbed the vase and flowers from Nick. The water from the vase went flying out, narrowly missing Nick, who stepped back in time. "Sorry! *Trudy!*"

"Yes, Sheriff?" Trudy responded with an innocence that was touching.

"Let's just put these out here, please?"

"Yes, ma'am."

"You know I'm—I'm—" She sneezed three times in rapid succession. "Allergic to roses." She sneezed again a few more times.

Trudy took the flowers. "I'm sorry, Sheriff. I forgot. I guess Jack Winter forgot, too, huh?"

"Jack Winter, the DA?" Ernie asked with his eyebrows raised. "He sent you flowers?"

"He's courting the sheriff," Ed said with a frown.

"Jack Winter?" Ernie asked again in disbelief. "The man's old enough to be your daddy!"

Sharyn glared at them. "Let's go back into the conference room," she suggested, sniffling.

Nick glared back at her as she passed him to go into the conference room. "Thought he made your skin crawl? Or did you mean that in a *good* way?"

"If we could stick to the subject," Sharyn suggested, sitting at the end of the scarred table.

"Okay, Sheriff," Ed said. "What are you doing to discourage that creep?"

"*That* isn't the subject." She grabbed a tissue and buried her nose in it. Then she looked at Nick, defying him to speak of anything but what he knew about Darva Richmond. "Well?"

Nick took a deep breath and put his notebook on the table. "As I was going to say before I was interrupted by your personal life, I cheated. I had a feeling you'd want to go ahead with the autopsy so I sent toxicology away yesterday. I finished the preliminary report on my findings this morning."

"And?" she demanded.

"Darva Richmond was killed by something besides a bear. She had strychnine in her body. Probably rat poison. That's what actually killed her. There were no contusions that I could find from the back of the head or neck. The face and throat tissue were mostly gone so that was the best I could do. She was covered in honey. Interestingly enough, the sheriff brought up the idea that perhaps Darva and her husband had been playing around with the honey, but the honey was on the outside of her clothes and in her hair. Traces were there on what was left of her face."

"Honey?" Ed asked.

"Yeah. Plain old garden variety except for one thing." He took out a small bottle from the local hardware store. "I checked with Sam Two Rivers about this. He said it would be unlikely that the honey would be enough to draw the bear to the body, especially if it was already down. I found some stuff that hunters use to attract bears to certain spots. It was mixed with the honey on Darva's body."

"How long would it take for the strychnine to kill her?" Sharyn wondered.

"Not long," Nick answered. "Maybe thirty minutes. She would have lost consciousness, then gone into convulsions and stopped breathing."

"Why didn't the bear get sick that ate her?" Ernie asked.

"Sam Two Rivers said the mother bear was close to five hundred pounds. He said she probably didn't eat the body so much as play with it. It would've taken a lot higher dosage."

"So the husband had to do it!" Ed surmised. "They were up on the mountain alone that night."

"How was the poison administered?" Sharyn asked, not as ready to blame Donald Richmond.

"Apparently, the happy couple had wine and dinner, then went to bed. I'd say it was probably in the wine."

Sharyn considered the possibilities. None of them looked good for Donald Richmond. "Has that trailer been moved from the mountain yet?"

Ernie consulted his file. "Yesterday afternoon. It's in the impound lot."

Nick nodded. "I'll get a couple of students and we'll go over it. If we're lucky, they didn't drink all of the wine or eat all of the food."

Joe walked into the conference room and slapped Ed on the back. "Hey, Ernie! Good to see you!"

"Hi Joe," Ernie replied. "Good to see you, too."

"What's up?" the deputy wondered.

"Darva Richmond was murdered," Sharyn told him.

"Another murder? I thought she was killed by a bear?"

"It looks like someone used the bear attack to try to hide the real murder," she explained.

"The husband?"

"Looks that way," Ernie agreed.

"I'm finished with patrol," Joe told Sharyn. "You want me to jump in on this?"

Sharyn considered his request. "For now, let's let Nick find what he can in the trailer. I want to keep this between us until we get some more information. We know where to find Donald. Ernie and I talked to him this morning but I think we might have to see him again. I'd like you and Ed to go up and take a look around that site again."

"What are we looking for?" Joe wondered.

"Anything that you can find that might go along with this woman being killed, then set up for the bear to mutilate. When you get done, take a swing past the mansion and pick Donald up."

Joe nodded. "We'll keep it quiet, Sheriff."

"Good."

"Ernie, anything you can find about Darva and Donald Richmond's life before they came here. Darva still had her Montana driver's license in her wallet. Let's see what they were like before they came to Diamond Springs."

"You got it, Sheriff!"

They started walking out of the conference room.

"Ed tell you he and I are sharing a bachelor pad?" Joe asked Ernie.

Ernie glanced at Ed. "No. No, he didn't. I bet that's fun."

"Hey, it's great! Sarah's so stubborn. She thinks I have too much fun. She doesn't understand what the job is like. I need to relax."

"I hear you," Ernie sympathized, walking out with him.

Ed groaned and rolled his eyes at Sharyn. "Have you talked to Sarah yet?"

"No. I didn't say I would interfere!"

"He's ruining my life, Sheriff! One of us will be the next murder in Diamond Springs if he doesn't get out of my house!"

"Ed—"

"Maybe I can talk Ernie into taking him home."

"Ernie's got his own trouble with Annie right now."

"What am I gonna do?"

"I don't know!"

"Sharyn, can I talk to you?" Nick asked impatiently.

Ed swung around and left them with a sympathetic nod at Nick.

"Yes?" she asked, putting together the paperwork he'd given her on the autopsy. When he didn't answer, she looked up at him. "Nick?"

"What are you doing to discourage Winter?" he demanded.

"Does anyone around here know what a *private* life is?"

"So you're going out with him?"

"Nick," she told him openly. "It's none of your business!"

He looked as though he might say something else but he closed his notebook and marched out of the room without another word. Sharyn shook her head, took a deep breath, and followed him.

"Sheriff, Eleanore Lacey on the phone for you. Line two," Trudy said.

Sharyn closed her office door behind her. She sat at her father's desk and picked up the phone. "What can I do for you, Miss Lacey?"

"Sheriff, I have some letters that I think you should look at. They're from my niece. Could you come to the hotel? I'm sorry but my old bones just don't want to move around like they used to."

Sharyn glanced at her watch. "I can be there in a few minutes, Miss Lacey."

"Thank you, Sheriff. I know I sound like a silly old fool but did you ever just have a feeling that something was wrong?"

"All the time, ma'am. I'll be right over."

Nick was gone when Sharyn walked out of her office. The roses in the beautiful vase were on an empty desk in the center of the room. Trudy was on the phone. Ernie was in his office on the computer.

"I'm going to the hotel to talk to Miss Lacey," she told him.

"Miz Eleanore," Ernie corrected her with a smile, not looking up from his computer. "Why?"

"She called and said she brought some letters from her niece. I guess she thinks they explain something about Darva being murdered."

"Want me to tag along?"

"No, that's okay. We need that information more than I need help talking to an old lady. Maybe she's really got something. After Nick's findings, maybe she has something that can place Donald as the killer."

"That seems a little unlikely."

"And too easy?"

"You said it, I didn't."

"Ernie, do you really think Jack Winter is as bad as everyone paints him?"

He did look up at her then. "Worse. If you were my daughter, I'd tell you to stay clear away from him. The man is purely evil. Someday, the devil's gonna come after his own."

Sharyn felt a cold chill spread up her spine at his words. "I know no one believes it, but I'm not interested in seeing him any more than I have to see him."

"I believe it."

She looked at him curiously. "Why?"

Ernie applied himself to the computer again. "Because I have faith in the power of love. After thirty years, Annie and I found our way back together. You'll find the right man for you, too."

"I wish he'd come along before my mother's engagement party."

Ernie laughed. "Who said he hasn't come along already?"

Sharyn held up her hand. "I'm going to The Regency. I'll be back later."

"Yes, ma'am."

The weather was brisk again but the sun was warm. The deep blue sky that only came with the colder temperatures silhouetted the grand form of The Regency Hotel against its majestic background.

The hotel had been built back in the twenties when for a brief period, Diamond Springs (known as Palmer in those days) had lived through a heyday of rich visitors. The hotel, along with the playhouse across the street, had been built to accommodate them.

The architect had created both buildings to withstand the ravages of time and weather with equal grace. Both were still being used for their original purposes, though the rich and famous had moved on a long time before. A few white blossoms still clung to a cherry tree near the front door of The Regency. The building had sheltered the tree from the lake and mountain breezes, the same way it would give shelter to her mother's engagement party in a little less than two weeks. Even illness wouldn't save Sharyn from the event. Her mother would only see it as another way to show her dislike for Senator Talbot. She was going to have to be there for that night, along with a few hundred other guests from across the country. The senator had far-reaching fingers.

Sharyn smiled at the concierge. He nodded to her and smiled. She walked into the huge foyer with the chandelier hanging sixty feet above her head. As a child, she'd been afraid it might fall on her. She had stepped quickly on the red carpet when she'd been there.

"I'm looking for Eleanore Lacey," she told the desk clerk.

"Of course, Sheriff," the man replied quietly. "Room 307. Not going to arrest her here, are you?"

Sharyn smiled. "I don't plan to arrest anyone today, Mr. Bartlett. But if I do, I'll be discreet."

The manager smiled. "We'll be seeing you here for the senator's engagement party, I believe?"

"That's right," she replied. "Thank you." Sharyn didn't wait around to hear if the man had any ideas on who she should bring as her date.

The ride was fast and smooth in the ornate elevators. Sharyn stepped out onto more red carpeting and followed the hall down to Room 307. She knocked softly and opened the door when a voice called for her to enter. Miss Eleanore was sitting on a love seat, her legs covered by a warm throw. The old lady looked like a queen on her throne. Sharyn took off her hat and took a seat when the gracious hand waved to her.

"Thank you for coming, Sheriff. I know you're busy. But

I found these letters from Darva. I brought them with me for comfort but I actually had forgotten what they said. They weren't at all comforting."

Sharyn took the letters from the old lady. She smelled the cloying rose scent and moved away quickly. "Thanks. You said that you and Mrs. Richmond were close?"

"Yes. In Montana, we saw each other frequently. Once she came here with Donald, it was different."

"Did you talk to her while she was here?"

"Yes, of course. On the phone. She was troubled by the people around her at the house where they were staying. She said they were mean and spiteful and she didn't know if Donald would get the money or not."

Sharyn glanced at the first letter and frowned. The postmark said that it had been mailed from Diamond Springs three months earlier. "Your niece was certainly unhappy here."

Eleanore Lacey stared down at the plaid blanket that covered her legs. She pleated the soft material between her fingers. "Darva had a hard life, Sheriff. Her parents died when she was very young and I raised her. She was such a precocious child! She loved to have an audience! I think that's why she went on the stage later. She had a nice career already when she met Donald. I think she was sorry that she married him."

"But he had some money and the promise of more to come?"

Sharyn's biting tone brought the old lady's head up. "I think she loved him when she first married him. But in the five years that followed, there were hard feelings between them."

Both letters were full of talk about how terrible it was for Darva in Diamond Springs. Meeting Tad Willis, a local gallery owner, had helped but she wanted to go back to

Montana. Sharyn noticed a pattern in the subsequent letters where Tad Willis was mentioned frequently.

"Did your niece ever say anything about wanting to leave her husband?"

"No." Eleanore frowned. "Something's happened, hasn't it? You know something more you haven't told me, Sheriff."

"You're very perceptive, ma'am. The medical examiner just informed me that you might be right. Your niece might have been murdered. We'll be investigating her death as a homicide."

"Oh no!" Eleanore gasped. "I knew it. I just knew it! I—I didn't want to think about it. It was terrible enough that she would be hurt by a bear, but murdered! Who could have done this?"

"I don't know yet, ma'am," Sharyn admitted. "That's why we're investigating. It might take us some time to sort through the whole thing, but we'll find her killer."

"It was him," Miss Eleanore remarked bitterly.

"Him?"

"Donald, of course! He has a terrible temper! He was always jealous of her. If another man even looked at her, he went crazy! Darva loved him. He had nothing to worry about but you know how that doesn't make some people feel any better? You know how it is to be young and in love. People, especially men, say and do silly things when they're in love."

"Yes, ma'am. The question is: was Donald jealous of Tad Willis and the time he spent with his wife?"

"I don't know. Darva was always very subdued on the phone, like she felt those people were watching her. She didn't mention it to me. She only spoke of it in these letters. Do you know who this man is?"

"Yes, ma'am. I'll talk to him. If I find out anything, I'll let you know."

"Thank you, Sheriff," Eleanore said with a trembling smile. "I know Darva is in good hands."

"Thank you, ma'am, for bringing this to my attention." The other woman's rose scent slid into Sharyn's senses and she started sneezing. "I'll get back to you." She sneezed again and again. "As soon as I can."

Sharyn left the room, sneezing. As a child, she'd had to have shots during the summer for her rose allergy. Her mother's rose garden, just outside their door, had been a constant source of irritation. She had been hoping to outgrow the problem. Mostly, she just stayed away from them as much as possible.

Unfortunately, roses seemed to be the preferred flower at banquets and fundraising dinners. She usually went into those affairs fine but came out sneezing. The banquet where she'd met Darva and Donald Richmond had been a fiasco. There had been a huge spray of roses and chrysanthemum right on the podium. She'd had to cut short her speech on law enforcement in the twenty-first century because she couldn't stop sneezing.

It was unusual for her to be allergic to a perfume. Maybe it was distilled from the essential oils, she considered, making her way back to the office. She didn't have a problem with one rose. But a host of them sent her into sneezing fits. Apparently, Eleanore Lacey's perfume was like a dozen or more roses! She hoped Darva's death was cleared up quickly.

Considering the information Eleanore Lacey had given her, Sharyn walked into the office, ready to go to work. Obviously, there were forces in Darva's life that no one else knew about. Normally, these things would never be known, but in a murder investigation, privacy wasn't an option.

"Sheriff, your mother just called," Trudy said. "She

wants to know if you can meet her and Kristie for lunch at Morrison's."

Sharyn took off her coat and glanced at her watch. "What time?"

"Noon."

"Call her back for me, Trudy. Tell her I'll be there, please."

"Sure thing," the woman replied. "What's up?"

"How do you know something's up?"

"I know *you!*"

"Never mind! Has Ernie gone out yet?"

"Not yet," Ernie said, coming out of his office. "What's up?"

Trudy laughed and dialed Faye Howard's phone number.

"In here," Sharyn said, opening her office door.

They barely got settled when David knocked on the door. "Sheriff? I need to talk to you."

"I want to talk to you, too," Sharyn answered. "Come in and close the door."

David looked at her warily and then turned to Ernie. "What did I do now?"

Ernie smiled and shook his head. "You're paranoid, son! Nobody said you did anything."

"It's true, David," Sharyn said. "I want to talk to you about Julia and her relatives."

"Oh." David shook his head. "That's what I wanted to talk to you about, too."

"What?"

David fidgeted in his chair. "I need some time off. Julia's broken up with me for good. She didn't want to leave the mansion and live with me. I need a few days of personal time."

"I wish I could give it to you but I need you out with JP until he learns the ropes. Especially since we're going to be investigating Darva Richmond's death as a homicide."

"A homicide?"

"Preliminary autopsy results pointed to her death not being an accident," she explained. "The family was pretty hard on her and Donald."

"But what would they have to gain by killing Darva?" David wondered. "They'd need to kill Donald."

"Mr. Richmond told us this morning that he was thinking about dropping the challenge to the will because of Darva's death," Ernie said calmly. "I think the sheriff wants to talk to you about Julia's family being involved."

David stared at both of them. "You really think one of them could have killed Darva?"

"That's what we're asking you," Sharyn told him. "You've spent time over there. We've already heard that it was pretty tense in the mansion with Darva and Donald staying there. Do you think Julia or one of her family would be capable of killing her?"

"No way! Not Julia anyway!"

Ernie glanced at Sharyn and shook his head. "Maybe you could think like a deputy instead of a lovesick calf?"

"Hey!" David turned on him. "At least I didn't quit the job to be with Julia!"

"Okay, that's enough!" Sharyn shut him down. "I just want your opinion on the family. What about her parents?"

David glared at Ernie. "Both of her parents are crazy, Sharyn. I wouldn't put anything past them. They didn't think I was good enough for Julia. I think they just didn't want me there so they could take over the estate. Julia is still heartbroken from Beau's death. She isn't thinking clearly. If anyone could be responsible, it would be Amanda and Skeeter."

"Skeeter?"

"Yeah," David replied. "They had Julia pay off all of

their bills. She bought them a new car and sent them for a long trip on a yacht. They want to tell her everything she should do. And not do."

"Okay." Sharyn took notes in her small notepad.

"Want me to bring them in or go out to the mansion and interrogate them?"

"Neither," she said firmly. "You're too close to be directly involved with the investigation. One of us will handle it."

David nodded. His light-brown hair was sticking up all over his head and he needed a shave. "What about my time off?"

"Not this time, David. You'll have to struggle through. I need you."

"Okay, Sharyn. I'll do the best I can." He stood up to walk out. "Will you let me know about Julia's parents? With them out of the picture, she'd probably take me back."

Sharyn smiled at him. "Go home and get some rest, David. I'll let you know if anything changes."

"Thanks."

Ernie stood to walk out, too.

"Ernie?" Sharyn asked. "Will you stay?"

"Just be a minute," Ernie said quickly, following David from the office. He was true to his word and only gone a moment. He took his seat again. "So, what did Miz Eleanore have to say?"

Sharyn glanced towards the door. "What's going on?"

"Nothing," Ernie said quickly. "Just a friendly word of advice for David."

"Advice to the love worn?" Sharyn quipped.

"Pretty much."

She sat back in her chair. "Miss Eleanore brought two letters from her niece. Darva was spending a lot of time with Tad Willis. She says Donald was the jealous type."

Ernie thought about it. "I know I've heard the name but—"

"He's the one that opened the gallery down by the lake in the old train station," she supplied.

"Oh, right! Darva Richmond was involved with him?"

"I'm not sure yet. This letter," she passed it to him, "was postmarked last month. Miss Eleanore said Donald was jealous of all of Darva's male friends but that she loved him too much to fool around."

"So, we go back to Donald Richmond again?"

"Looks like it. With this letter and the aunt telling us that Donald had a temper that flared when he was jealous, combined with the fact that the poison worked in thirty minutes. It almost has to be Donald."

Ernie shook his head as he skimmed through the emotional letter. "I'm still not convinced. I don't know. He just doesn't seem the type."

"We're going to have to go down and talk to Tad Willis and get his take on all of this. Then I guess we'll talk to Amanda and Skeeter out at the mansion. Since Ed and Joe are already bringing Donald in this afternoon, we should have some answers."

"I guess so. I put a call in to an editor at the *Evening Trib*. That's the newspaper for Elkton, Montana, where the Richmonds lived before they came here to annoy Skeeter and Amanda. There was no record for either of them. Not even a wild party or a parking ticket. They kept a low profile out there."

"Well, it wasn't Donald's hometown," Sharyn suggested. "Maybe he blossomed here."

"Maybe so," Ernie agreed. "Are you gonna go to lunch with your mama and your sister?"

"Yes. Want to come?"

Ernie saw the desperation in Sharyn's blue eyes and couldn't say no. It reminded him of her daddy. T. Raymond was always desperate when it came to understanding Faye. "Just let me get my jacket."

"Great! Thanks!"

They were walking out of her office together when Sharyn looked up and saw Annie at Trudy's desk. "Maybe not," she said, nudging Ernie.

"Maybe not," he agreed, his brown eyes suddenly full of nothing but Annie. "Would you mind, Sheriff?"

"Not at all, Ernie," she answered with a smile that she hoped was enough to convince him. "Hi, Annie."

"Hello, Sharyn. How are you?"

"Fine. How are you?"

"All right, I guess. I wanted to talk to Ernie." Her eyes were clinging to him.

"I was just going to lunch," Sharyn replied. She glanced at Ernie. She hoped he wasn't going away again with Annie but if he did, she would understand. She knew he loved his job but she also knew that Annie was the love of his life. "I'll see you both later."

Chapter Five

Ernie and Annie walked out together while Sharyn got her jacket. Trudy was beaming as she watched them go out the door together. "They are so made for each other."

"I know."

"I don't know how Ernie could let her go for this job!"

"He'd have to do something to make a living," Sharyn reminded her.

"Yes, but he could do something that made sense! You know that whole Jefferson school thing almost killed him! It almost killed me and nobody was after me!"

Sharyn smiled. "I know, Trudy."

"This is a crazy job for crazy people." She looked at Sharyn. "You should give it up, too, Sheriff."

"I know. We all should," Sharyn remarked. "That's why you've been here for ten years."

Trudy sighed. "I know. I'm as crazy as the rest of you. Ben is always telling me that I should quit."

Sharyn thought about Trudy's husband. "But he's a stock car driver! How can he think what you do is crazy?"

"I don't know," Trudy admitted. "Because what he does is totally insane! We both know it! But two more years and he figures he can make enough money to retire. That's what we're waiting for. We already put money down on a big Winnebago. We're gonna travel around the country and watch other people do crazy things!"

"Sounds good."

"Ernie took David down a peg or two!"

"When?"

"Out here before," Trudy confided. "Told the boy he'd better start giving you some respect unless he wanted Ernie to have a talk with his uncle and the two of them would sort him out. David said yes sir, and hightailed it out of here."

"I wish he wouldn't do that. David is going to have to learn to work with me."

Trudy smiled until her dimples were showing. She pushed her unruly hair back out of her face. "You mean before Ernie and Joe bust him down? I agree. But he's a stubborn boy! Always was!"

"Trudy—"

"Aren't you late for lunch?"

Sharyn took a deep breath and left her there at her desk. The phone rang and she ducked out of the office. The sun was warm on her head and the cool wind was crisp and invigorating. In another month, it would be spring for real and the weather would turn warm. The dogwood trees along the street would flower and the roses would start to bloom. Tourists would line the streets again, filling the lake with their boats. Another season would change and life would go on.

She walked right into Nick, who was coming up the stairs to the office. He put a gloved hand on both of her arms. "Whoa! Where's the fire?"

"Late for lunch with my mother," she confided. "Why are you out here instead of in back?"

"I'm just coming from a class. You can't afford me full time, you know."

"I guess that's true," she agreed. Nick taught forensics and psychology at the college as well as working as the county medical examiner.

"I left the kids with it, though. They're sorting, tagging, and bagging. It's good experience for them."

"You need an assistant."

"Considering my last choice for assistant, I don't think so." He walked down the stairs and fell in stride with her.

"You could make a better choice."

"I could," he admitted. "But where would the fun be in that? He was just making sure there was plenty of work for me."

"Nick!"

"Okay, sorry! It was just a little ME humor."

"Where are you going?" she wondered as he continued to walk with her down the crowded sidewalk.

"With you. I was coming to have you buy me lunch."

"Oh."

He looked at her and laughed. "Oh? Is that it?"

"What did you want me to say?"

" 'Get lost, Nick. I don't need you tagging along. I'm meeting Jack Winter for a secret tryst.' "

"Will you get off that Jack Winter thing?" she demanded. "I'm really not involved with him except on a professional level."

"Yeah. All of your colleagues send you roses every day."

"Thank goodness they don't! I wouldn't be able to breathe!"

"That was pretty stupid of him," he said thoughtfully, grateful that the other man had made the mistake and not him. "So, why aren't you complaining about me going with you?"

Sharyn grimaced. "I'd take the devil himself with me to lunch today if he wanted to go. My mother got her engagement ring from Caison. She wants me to see it."

"I don't mind the comparison and I understand the sentiment behind it." He tucked her arm into his. "Consider me the devil himself, Sheriff Howard. Glad to help out."

Sharyn laughed as they walked down the street together, arm in arm. The wind whipped her penny-bright hair, some of the longer strands almost touching the black strands of Nick's hair. A noisy car passed and they bent their heads close together as they continued speaking.

To a causal observer, they looked like more than friends. Jack Winter sipped his brandy, looking down at them from his office window in the old courthouse. He turned as Lennie Albert brought in his lunch on a tray. "Find out what you can about Nick Thomopolis, will you?"

"Sir?" Lennie asked, putting down the tray on the cloth-covered table.

"The medical examiner," Jack Winter said again. "I want to know about him."

Lennie swallowed hard. "Yes, sir."

Faye Howard started to berate her daughter for being late, as usual, until she saw Nick Thomopolis at her side. "Sharyn! You look radiant!" she gushed instead, kissing Sharyn's cheek. "Nick! I'm so happy to see you!"

"Faye," Nick acknowledged her as she kissed his cheek. He held out his hand to Caison Talbot. "Senator."

"Nick! Good to see you!" The senator was tan and fit, the shock of his thick white hair emphasizing the deep blue of his eyes. He had a strong Southern drawl that he used when it was appropriate. "Glad to see you could make it, Sharyn."

Sharyn nodded but didn't reply.

"Hi Nick," Kristie said quickly. "This is Keith Reynolds. Keith, this is Nick Thomopolis, the county medical examiner."

"Wow! Glad to meet you, sir!" Keith said, standing to take Nick's hand. He was a thin, angular boy with a high forehead and an already receding hairline. "I've been thinking about becoming an ME."

"Really?" Nick glanced at Sharyn as he took her jacket. He put both their coats on a nearby chair. "We could use an assistant in the office. Taken any courses?" He held Sharyn's chair for her to sit down, smiling at her while she frowned at him.

"Only some drama and political science. I haven't decided on my major yet," Keith replied. He smiled at Kristie. "We're thinking about transferring here together this fall."

Sharyn and Faye Howard both looked pointedly at Kristie.

"We're just thinking about it!" She made a face at both of them.

"You've done very well at State," Faye reminded her younger, prettier daughter, who looked so much like her in her youth with her burnished blond hair and big blue eyes.

"Where are you going to school, Keith?" Sharyn asked, wondering if something was wrong with her since she was going to say the same thing as her mother. It was scary.

"I'm at Duke right now, ma'am. But it's a long way from home and I've been thinking about being closer." He smiled at Kristie and they all knew who he wanted to be closer to.

"Both fine schools!" Caison interjected. "Nick, have a drink with me!"

"Thanks, Senator," Nick answered. "But I'm working."

"Oh, really? I wouldn't think there was much to work on with that girl who got eaten by the bear!"

"Caison!" Faye said, her hand to her heart that was pumping beneath her lilac silk dress. "Please! Not at lunch!"

"Actually, Senator, it looks like it might be a murder," Nick replied.

Sharyn shook her head but it was too late.

"Did someone train the bear to kill the woman?" Kristie asked ingenuously.

"Of course not!" Faye Howard responded firmly. "I had twenty years of such dinner table talk with T. Raymond, Caison! I will not put up with it anymore! It's all Sharyn lives and breathes, which is why she still doesn't have a date for our engagement party! I think we're here for something much finer!" She held out her hand and the big diamond sparkled in the light.

"Mom!" Kristie protested on her sister's behalf. "Sharyn works hard for Diamond Springs."

"I know she does, dear. And I'm sure one of the men in that nice new jail they built would be pleased to bring her to the party!"

Sharyn was about to get to her feet when Nick reached over and took her hand. "Actually, Faye, I asked Sharyn to go to your engagement party with me."

Sharyn's mother smiled broadly. "Nick! You are the best! Whatever happened to that lovely woman we met a few months ago with you? Tiger or something?"

"Tigre," he replied, still holding Sharyn's hand even though her grip was breaking his fingers. "She was only here a few nights. She's back in New York."

Faye's delicate laugh tinkled across the table. "You're going to have to settle down soon, Nick. T. Raymond wouldn't like you dallying with his daughter between models!"

"*Mother!*" Sharyn couldn't hold it in any longer. "What are you saying?"

Faye smiled at her. "I'm just looking after your interests, Sharyn. Calm down."

"Mom!" Kristie added her own voice.

"Oh, for goodness' sake, hush!" Faye told her brightly. "And let's order lunch!"

The ordeal lasted almost an hour. Sharyn didn't eat much of her salad and she finally made an excuse to leave.

"Come and talk to me over the summer break if you're interested in working with the ME's office," Nick said to Keith.

"Thank you, sir." He took Nick's card. "I'll do that."

"Nice to see you again, Kristie." Nick smiled at Sharyn's younger sister.

"You, too, Nick!" She glanced at Sharyn then back to him. "See you at the party?"

"You bet."

"That was only less painful than having my arms pulled out," Sharyn remarked as she and Nick left the restaurant together. "Why do I ever agree to go out with them?"

"Because they're your family," he answered, shrugging into his coat. "You let her do that to you."

"What?" she demanded as they walked out into the sunshine together.

"You give her every opportunity to talk to you like a child. She just takes you up on it."

"Psychology 101?"

"Observation of you and your mother," he answered firmly. "She knows she can say things like that and how you're going to react. You let her get to you."

She glanced at him. "Is that why you told her you were going with me to the party?"

He didn't reply for a moment as they walked up the sidewalk towards the office. "No," he said finally. "I'm too selfish for that and I don't really care about your weird relationship with your mother."

"What does that mean?" she asked, stopping.

"It means, I wouldn't have said that if I didn't want to go with you to the party!" He turned to face her. The wind pushed her bright hair in and out of her eyes. He put his hands in his pockets to keep from putting them on her face. "It means that I've been trying to find a way to ask you to go for a few days. But you told me that you were worried about the rumors so I've kept my mouth shut."

Sharyn didn't know what to say. It didn't happen often that she ran out of words but this was one of those times. "This doesn't have to be a personal thing," she blurted out before her mind was fully connected to her mouth. Her heart was racing and her pride was on her sleeve. "I mean, we work together. People who work together can go out, even to parties. It happens all the time."

He stared at her. His black eyes became angry and his face echoed the distance he put between them. "That's right, Sharyn. It doesn't have to be personal! In fact, it doesn't have to be at all. Just because I said it, doesn't mean it has to happen!"

He started walking away from her and she shook her head. "What's wrong with you now?"

"You're a smart, problem-solving cop," he yelled without looking back at her. "You figure it out!"

Sharyn gave up and started up the stairs to the office after him. She would never understand Nick Thomopolis if she lived a hundred years and he tormented her every one of them! She was just trying to give him a chance to back out if he found someone else to go with that night. Someone he *did* have a personal relationship with. What was wrong with that?

Ernie met her on the stairs. "I've got a car coming around front," he told her. "I think we should see Tad Willis first, don't you?"

"Sure," she agreed. "How did it go with Annie?"

"Great!" He grinned at her, his eyes gleaming. "We're going to get back together and work on it. She understands how important the job is to me. I promised not to take any unnecessary chances. We're thinking about getting married when her divorce is final."

Sharyn hugged him. "That's wonderful, Ernie! I'm so happy for you!"

He looked at her critically. "How was lunch?"

"Don't ask!"

Charlie brought the sheriff's car around the building and pulled up close to the curb.

"Your mama acting up again?" he queried.

"Yes. And no. Nothing I didn't expect from her." She turned to him. "It was Nick, Ernie! I don't understand him."

"Sheriff, that's a whole other story," Ernie told her plainly. "I'd rather sort out a murder than go there!"

"So, you agree that he's crazy?"

He laughed. "I agree that you're both in need of guidance, ma'am. I'm just not the person to give it to you! I wish your daddy was still alive. He'd put you both straight in a heartbeat!"

"Sorry, it took so long to come around, Sheriff," Charlie apologized. "Between the new building and those forensic students tearing everything apart, I just don't know!"

"That's okay, Charlie," she told him with a smile. "Thanks."

"Good luck, Sheriff. Deputy."

Tad Willis's new gallery, which featured works by Southern artists, was housed in the old railroad station. Its pointed red roof and brown brick walls were covered in posters for a new exhibit of homespun quilts and loom-made clothing. Sharyn and Ernie parked outside the front door in the no-parking zone. They had barely left the car when Tad came out of the ornate red door.

"You can't park there!" he told them. "That's reserved

for loading and unloading." He was a short, thin man with a sallow face and round metal-framed glasses. He was waving his arms. His red suspenders jiggled as he moved.

"Slow down," Ernie told him firmly. "This is sheriff's business. We shouldn't need more than a few minutes of your time."

"I don't even have a few minutes right now," Tad replied quickly.

"You either have a few minutes here or at the office," Sharyn said. "Your choice."

"If this is about the parking tickets I haven't paid—"

"This is about a homicide investigation," Sharyn responded. A few people walked by, staring at the threesome, hoping to hear some tidbit of gossip to carry back home. "I don't think you want to answer these questions on the street, sir."

Tad pushed his spectacles back on his face. "You're right, of course, Sheriff. I'm sorry. Come inside."

"This is art?" Ernie whispered, walking in beside Sharyn. Three big quilts hung over their heads, suspended from the ceiling by wires.

"It is if you like it," she answered with a smile.

He shrugged. "My mama used to call these bedcovers. We washed 'em and we put 'em back on the bed. Art is paintings of General Custer's Last Stand and the Mona Lisa."

Sharyn laughed, then sobered as Tad looked back at her. They sat down in his cramped office. Ernie and Sharyn took out their notepads.

"What's this all about, Sheriff?" Tad wondered.

"We need to ask you some questions about your relationship with Darva Richmond."

"Darva." He cleared his throat. "Mrs. Richmond has been an extremely generous patroness."

"Patroness?" Ernie asked.

"She contributed to the gallery. She did fundraising and also helped me find new artists."

"What about your personal relationship?" Sharyn wondered.

Tad shook his head. "We didn't have a personal relationship, per se, Sheriff. She was married. So am I."

Sharyn glanced at Ernie. "I know you've read about Mrs. Richmond's death by now, Mr. Willis."

"Yes, I have. What a terrible tragedy."

"Well, we have some of her letters. They're pretty descriptive. Were you having an affair?"

"What?" Tad was on his feet in an instant. "You had no right! You can't read her personal letters because she's dead! I'm going to file a lawsuit!"

"Sit down, Mr. Willis," Ernie said flatly. "We can do pretty much anything that needs to be done during a murder investigation."

"Murder?" he whimpered, resuming his seat. "What are you saying?"

"We're saying that Mrs. Richmond's death wasn't an accident, Mr. Willis," Sharyn explained. "We have reason to believe she was murdered."

Tad glanced between them. "So, why are you here? You think . . . you think I killed her? How? By using a bear to attack her?"

"She was poisoned, sir," Ernie told him. "The killer poured honey on her body to make us think she was attacked and killed by a bear."

"That's not possible! Who would do such a terrible thing?"

Sharyn studied his flushed face. "Maybe a jealous lover."

"A . . . lover? Me? You mean *me*?"

"Did you see Mrs. Richmond on Saturday?"

"No," Tad admitted. "It might make me seem more guilty, but she broke it off with me last week. She told me that her husband was suspicious and that she didn't want him to find out. She said it would ruin everything between them. She was pretty hot for the Richmond money. She wouldn't have done anything to mess that up."

"Did she say anything else?"

"She said that her husband was jealous when she talked to another man. She said they had big fights about it. She told me that he'd caught her with a lover once before and that he'd almost killed her." Tad took off his spectacles and wiped them on his shirt. "She told me that he *did* kill her lover. I didn't want to see her after that anyway."

"When was the last time you saw her?" Ernie questioned.

"The week before last. She came over here and we were . . . together. She called me to break it off because she was afraid of her husband."

"And where were you Sunday night?"

"At home. With my wife and kids."

Sharyn frowned. "Do you think Darva was more afraid of her husband finding out because he might hurt her or because he might cut her off from the Richmond trust fund?"

Tad shook his head. "Knowing Darva, it would be hard to say. I do think she was afraid of him but that probably added spice to her cheating. She would've done anything for the money."

"One more question," Sharyn insisted. "Did you love her?"

Tad shook his head. "I don't think so. I wouldn't have left my wife for her. It was just something that happened between us. It was fun for a few months, you know? Will my name have to be in the paper for this? My wife would be very hurt by it."

"We'll do what we can," Sharyn promised him, though it left a bitter taste in her mouth. "But the investigation is a matter of public record. I can't make any promises."

"Oh no!"

"Don't make any travel plans until you hear from us, Mr. Willis," Ernie told him shortly. "We could need to talk to you again. Or you might have to testify in court."

"This can't be happening to me!" Tad groaned as they left him. "I don't know what to do."

"Call your wife, son," Ernie counseled. "Tell her the truth like a man before she finds out from someone else."

"Well?" Sharyn asked Ernie as they climbed back into the car.

Ernie shook his head. "I don't know. He didn't sound devastated by her death but how would he have killed her? He sure wasn't there in the trailer with Donald and Darva! And I don't think he'd mention his wife as his alibi if he didn't have to."

"But someone could have put the poison in the wine at any time," Sharyn countered.

"Why wouldn't Donald be dead, too then?" Ernie questioned. "Same thing for the food. If either one was poisoned by someone else, wouldn't he be dead, too?"

"Maybe he didn't eat or drink anything."

"I hate to say it, Sheriff, but I think we were wrong about Donald Richmond. I think he might have found out about his wife having an affair with Tad Willis. This time, he killed her."

"What did you think about Tad saying that Donald had killed Darva's other lover?"

"I don't know," Ernie admitted. "Could've just been talk. It would've happened in Montana, I guess. We'd need the name of the man, if he existed. Maybe something will come in from that editor I queried."

"Let's hope so," she said. "I still have a hard time believing that Donald deliberately and cold-bloodedly killed his wife and another man. He just doesn't seem the type."

"Although he could be a psycho," Ernie suggested.

"We're seeing one part of his personality but he could have other crazy things going on in his head."

"Let's take a drive out to the mansion anyway. Ed and Joe should have Donald at the office by now. Let's give him time to think and give Nick time to find something in the food or wine. I'd like to hear what Julia's parents have to say anyway."

"You mean Amanda and Skeeter, who just want to persecute poor David?"

"Unlike you, Ernie, who just want to teach him some respect?"

Ernie glanced at her as he drove. "I'm not apologizing. I'm the head deputy. That boy needs some straightening out. He's about as crooked as a used nail right now. I haven't been away that long!"

Sharyn sighed. "David and I have our own struggle, Ernie."

"You mean that whole thing about you being sheriff without being deputy first? I've been a deputy for almost twenty-five years. If I don't mind, why should he? It's not like he was gonna be sheriff if you weren't!"

"Don't you ever mind, really?" She looked at his thin face and the sprig of hair on his head.

"Not once." He shook his head. "I'm not the type to be sheriff. I wouldn't want to handle all the political stuff you do. You make it look easy but I know you hate it, too. Think you'll run again?"

"I don't know," she admitted. "I suppose I will unless somebody has me removed from office before then."

"You know you've got my vote, Sheriff."

"Thanks, Ernie."

They stopped at the guard gate at the end of the Richmond estate. "Sheriff Sharyn Howard to see Julia Richmond."

The guard conveyed the message, then waved them through as the tall, iron gates opened.

"What a place, huh?" Sharyn said as they drove down the long, winding drive.

"Nice to look at," Ernie quipped. "But I'll take what I've got. Like being sheriff, there's just too much upkeep!"

Sharyn laughed. There was a platoon of grounds keepers in the woods around them, cutting dead branches and picking up debris from the winter storms. It would be a lot to keep up with, she decided, looking around her as they reached the big old Tudor mansion. Not that it mattered. People didn't have mansions on a sheriff's pay.

"Sheriff! Deputy Watkins!" Julia greeted them at the door. "I'm so glad to see you."

"Thank you, ma'am," Sharyn said with a smile. "I'm sorry we have to be here about another tragedy."

"Oh no!" Julia said, her face draining of all color. "What's happened?"

Ernie scratched his head. "Your—er—sister-in-law died, ma'am?"

"Oh, yes," Julia recalled. "That tragedy."

"We'd like to ask you a few questions about Darva Richmond," Sharyn told her.

"I don't really know much about her, Sheriff."

"She was pushy, arrogant, rude, and without character!" Amanda Rosemont descended the long stairway in a crimson gown. Her hair, as dark as Julia's, was piled on her head. "We're better off now that she's dead!"

"Mama!" Julia chastised her. "Hush!"

"Don't hush me, Missy! I can speak my mind! I couldn't stand the woman! She pushed Donald into doing this. He wouldn't have done it on his own."

"Forty million dollars is a pretty powerful incentive, ma'am," Ernie suggested.

"It was that vixen, I'm telling you! She goaded him and

egged him into challenging the estate and making it difficult for all of us!"

"So, in other words, you're saying that you thought Donald would give up the challenge to the will if Darva was gone?" Sharyn asked bluntly.

"Yes," Amanda admitted. "That would be my guess. He said as much this morning after breakfast, didn't he, Julia?"

"Yes, I think he did, Sheriff."

"Of course, that could make you all suspects in her death," Sharyn continued.

"Suspects?" Julia wrinkled her pretty little nose.

Her mother slapped her arm. "How many times do I have to tell you not to do that? Wrinkles last forever!"

"Darva Richmond was murdered," Ernie told them both.

"And that makes us all suspects?" Amanda demanded.

"Darva was poisoned," Sharyn replied. "An easy way to kill someone. Especially someone pushy, arrogant, rude, and without character."

Amanda Rosemont wrinkled her own nose. "I know about you, Sheriff! I know how you trick people into confessing! You won't get me that easy!"

Ernie cleared his throat. "Ma'am? Are you saying you killed Darva Richmond?"

"I hated her," Amanda amended. "I didn't kill her. It was probably poor Donald. He probably couldn't live with her any more."

Julia was silent until her mother nudged her with her elbow. "Uh—yes. It could've been Donald."

"Did they argue? Did you think they had a bad relationship?"

"Well, sometimes," Julia admitted, glancing at her mother for guidance. "I heard them arguing at night about the money. Donald wanted to leave. Darva kept insisting they had to stay and get the money."

Sharyn stared at her. "Do you have any idea what perjury is, Mrs. Richmond?"

"I know what I heard," Julia repeated. "I heard them arguing about the money."

"So did I," her mother added. "All of us here heard them arguing about the money."

"What about another man?" Ernie asked.

"That witch!" Amanda screeched. "Like she could get another man!"

Sharyn's cell phone rang. "Excuse me, please." She walked away from them to answer while Ernie continued questioning the two women. "Sheriff Howard."

"I found it," Nick told her. "No clever disguise or attempt to hide it. The wine is laced with it."

"What kind of wine?" she asked, juggling her pen and paper with her phone.

"Domaine Leflaive burgundy 1959. A very good and expensive year."

"Thanks, Nick."

"That's what I'm here for, ma'am. Nothing personal."

The phone went dead. Sharyn closed it with a snap that made them all look at her. Amanda and Julia had been arguing with Ernie about their relationship with Darva and Donald. Skeeter had come downstairs and joined in, trying to support his wife and daughter without knowing what they were saying.

"I think we need to take a look at your wine cellar," Sharyn told them. "It seems that Darva drank poison with her wine."

"Don't you need a search warrant for that, Sheriff?" Skeeter asked. He was a wizened man, only half the size of his wife. He looked more like Julia, his features delicately drawn.

"If you don't want to agree to a search."

"If you've got something to hide," Ernie continued.

"We've got nothing to hide, Sheriff," Amanda assured her. "But I think we'll wait for that warrant while Julia makes a call to her lawyer."

"I have been through this before," Julia told her nervously.

"No, ma'am," Sharyn said. "You haven't been accused of a crime before."

Julia bit her lip. "Are you accusing me of killing Darva?"

"No, ma'am," Sharyn said carefully. "I don't think you have anything to hide. But what will it look like to everyone else when they hear about the warrant?"

Julia looked at her parents. "I'm going to let them search the house. We don't have anything to hide." She shrugged her dainty shoulders. "Go ahead, Sheriff. You won't need a warrant." She pointed out the wine cellar, then stepped aside.

"You're a fool, Julia!" her mother told her.

"Hush, Mama!"

"Did they used to call you slick when you were in school?" Ernie wondered as they walked down into the cellar. " 'Cause that was mighty slick."

"You know what they used to call me! How many times did you hear me tell my father the whole story when I came home from school?"

"You changed when you went away to college," he said quietly. "Is that why you want Kristie to stay at State?"

"Yes and no. She's too young to get involved that heavily with Keith."

"Not that you could stop her."

"I could arrest them both."

Ernie laughed. "I think your daddy wanted to do that with you a few times. It never works!"

"How'd you get so smart, Ernie?" she wondered as they looked through the racks of wine.

"Practice," he replied sagely. "Lots of practice. Whoa!

Here we go!" He blew the dust off a label. "Here's a missing bottle and the one beside of it is the same." He looked at the note Sharyn had again. "Domaine Leflaive burgundy 1959."

"Great. Let's take it with us." Sharyn saw a small sink in a corner and went to wash her hands. She looked on the shelf at eye level and saw a box of rat poison. Carefully, she put on latex gloves and got it down to read the side. "This contains strychnine."

Ernie frowned. "That's a little convenient."

"Maybe," Sharyn said. "Or maybe Amanda and Skeeter just weren't expecting company."

Chapter Six

"She didn't say you could take stuff out of here with you," Amanda protested as Ernie and Sharyn walked out of the mansion with the rat killer and the wine.

"What difference does it make?" Julia asked, tired of the whole thing. "None of us killed Darva, however much we might have wanted to."

"It's the principle," Skeeter told his daughter.

"Is there anything else you can tell us that might be helpful?" Ernie wondered.

"For instance, where all of you were Sunday night?" Sharyn suggested.

"Nothing I can think of," Julia answered quietly. "We were all here together. Is that an alibi?"

"If that's the truth, that's all that matters," Sharyn said.

"Thank you for not bringing the press into this." Julia swung her dark hair across her shoulder and held out her hand to Sharyn. "I really do hope you find who did this."

"We'll let you know," Ernie said with a curt nod. He got

into the sheriff's car beside Sharyn and grinned at her. "She even thanked *us* for searching her place. Slick!"

"I understand what David was saying about the parents." Sharyn shuddered. "I wouldn't have lived here, mansion or not."

"Guess Darva felt different."

"And Donald grew up here."

"Did you notice one thing?"

Sharyn nodded. "They didn't know about Darva sleeping with Tad Willis."

"Or they sure would have let us know! They didn't hear them arguing about it. They didn't even think Darva would be able to find another man who'd want her."

Sharyn glanced at him. "Which means what? We know from Tad Willis that he and Darva were having an affair. Miss Eleanore told us that Donald was jealous when Darva looked at another man. Tad went one step further and said Donald killed the first one. Maybe they just didn't argue about it."

Ernie fingered the place on his lip where his straggly mustache had been. "Maybe that's what threw us off about Donald. He's cool and calm and rational."

"All the traits of a psychotic personality."

"Exactly." Ernie glanced at her. "Where are we going with all of this?"

"I imagine we're arresting Donald Richmond for the murder of Darva Richmond."

"This poor family can't catch a break with a glove on, I swear! I hate this for them."

Sharyn called the DA's office from the car as they headed back into Diamond Springs. Five minutes later, Lennie was on the phone, telling her that Jack Winter wanted to see her. "I don't have time for this, Lennie! Put Mr. Winter on the phone!"

"Sorry," Lennie replied smoothly. "He's not in the office."

"Then how am I supposed to see him?"

"He'll be back by then."

Sharyn drummed her fingers on the dash. "Tell him I need that arrest warrant, Lennie! We're arresting Donald Richmond for his wife's murder. I expect to have it on my desk today!"

"I'll tell him, Sheriff," Lennie replied with a smile in his voice. "I can't make any guarantees, though."

"Just tell him what I said," she repeated, then closed the phone.

"Jack Winter's playing some deep game with you," Ernie said. "Be careful. Your daddy used to say that he'd rather go up against the devil himself than Jack Winter."

Sharyn smiled when she thought about Nick's words that afternoon. "Ernie, this doesn't have anything to do with Jack Winter, but what's wrong with Nick? He's back and forth, hot and cold. He asked me to go with him to my mother's engagement party, in front of my mother and Caison. I knew why he was doing it. He felt bad for me. But when I tried to tell him that I understood that it wasn't personal, he blew me off! I just don't understand that man!"

"That much is obvious."

"Will you stop being so cryptic about it? I have to work with him almost every day! What's the secret?"

Ernie shook his head. He pulled the sheriff's car into the lot behind the office and turned off the engine. "I'm telling you this as a friend of your family and a man who feels like your daddy since yours left, Sharyn."

"Yes?"

"Smell the coffee."

"Excuse me?"

"Wake up and smell the coffee."

"Ernie, what is that supposed to mean?"

"You'll have to figure it out. That's all I'm saying." They got out of the car and walked through and around the construction being done behind the office.

"How do you do that?" Sharyn asked him.

"Do what?"

"Turn that Sheriff/ma'am/Sharyn thing on and off. Don't you get confused?"

"No, ma'am."

She shook her head. "My father would've given me a better answer."

"And I'm sorry he's not here to set you straight on this. You're as close as I'm ever gonna come to a child of my own. I do the best I can for you."

"You do a pretty good job."

"Thank you."

"But I wish you'd come out with it!"

"Sorry."

David was pacing frantically, waiting for them outside the interrogation room. "Well? Did you go out to the mansion?"

"Yes," Sharyn replied. "We brought these back with us. Since you're here, you can run them over to the ME's office."

"What about Julia?"

"Are you asking if she knew anything about the murder?"

"No!" David declared. "I wanted to know if she mentioned *me!*"

"Take this stuff over to Nick!" Ernie said in disgust. "Then get cleaned up."

David was a mess. He hadn't shaved and his hair was

wild. He was still in the same uniform he'd been wearing for the past twenty-four hours. Except now it had ketchup and sleep creases in it. "Ernie!"

"I'm not telling you again, David! Get yourself together!"

Joe came out of the conference room and went to talk to his nephew. Ed walked out, too, but he stayed with Sharyn and Ernie.

"We picked up Richmond, no problem," Ed explained. "He's been crying like a baby for the last hour. If he's got something to say, I think he's probably ready to say it. Also, we found these." He held up two plastic bags.

"Where did you find them?" Sharyn asked. One of the bags held an empty jar of honey, without a top. The other held a scrap of material. "What's this?"

Ed shrugged. "We didn't know but it was with the jar in the dumpster about a few yards from the attack."

"This could be a piece of Darva's robe that we found her in. Let's get David to take this to Nick with the other stuff." Sharyn gave the bags back to Ed. "We found some rat poison with strychnine in it at the mansion in the wine cellar. Nick said the wine was laced with it. I called the DA for an arrest warrant." She looked towards Trudy's desk. "Trudy, did that warrant come in yet?"

"Not yet," Trudy told her.

"Okay. Let's read Mr. Richmond his rights and see how that goes. Maybe the warrant will be here by then," Sharyn decided. If Jack Winter's game cost her time on getting through this terrible thing with Donald Richmond, she was going to have something to say to Winter that would scorch the devil's ears! "Trudy, call Josh Hartsell for me, please."

"You think he needs a shrink?" Ed wondered, putting on his coat to catch up with Joe and David.

"I think he might," Sharyn said. "Let's go in."

Donald Richmond started crying again when he saw Sharyn.

"Mr. Richmond, I'm sorry we have to meet again like this."

"So am I, Sheriff. I didn't kill Darva! You have to believe me!"

Sharyn and Ernie sat down at the conference table.

"Mr. Richmond, before you say anything else, I think we should tell you your rights," Sharyn explained slowly. The man was almost incoherent. She wasn't sure how well any statement she got from him was going to stand up in court.

Ernie gave him his rights, including his right to an attorney. Donald waived them all, then started crying again.

"You do understand your rights, Mr. Richmond?" Ernie asked again.

"I do. I don't care."

"Will you sign here, please, sir." Ernie gave him a waiver to sign.

Donald signed it quickly. "I don't care about any of it. I didn't kill Darva!"

"She was poisoned, Mr. Richmond," Sharyn told him. "With rat poison."

"*No!*"

"Could you tell us if you ate or drank anything before you went to sleep that night in the trailer?" Sharyn asked him quietly.

"We had dinner," he replied. "We talked for a few minutes. Then we went to bed."

"What did you have to drink with dinner, Mr. Richmond?" Ernie questioned.

"I drank bottled water. Darva had wine. I'm allergic to wine." A dawning understanding came over his face. He ran his hand through his thick, blond hair. "It was the wine, wasn't it? The wine was poisoned! That's why she died and I didn't! I wish it would've been me! I wish I was dead!"

"The wine was a bottle from the mansion's cellars, sir. We found poison near the sink down there. I've given the box of poison to the ME, along with an empty jar of honey that we found in a dumpster at the park. It would be better to tell us now if your fingerprints are on those things."

"There's no way they could've been on it," he proclaimed. "I never went down there! I never touched that bottle! I can't drink wine. It had to be those harpies in that house! I warned Darva! I told her we should get out of there. She wouldn't listen."

Sharyn stopped writing. "You didn't want to pursue the challenge to the will?"

"*No!* We had some money. We wouldn't have been penniless but it wasn't enough for Darva. She was mad because we didn't get our fair share. She thought we should still be sole heir to everything."

"So you killed her," Ernie added.

"I didn't kill Darva! What will it take to convince you? I loved Darva! I would've done anything for her! I gave up my life for her!"

"What do you mean?" Sharyn wondered.

"I—I had a different life when I met Darva. I gave all that up for her. I came here because she wanted to have more. I wanted her to have more. But now those witches have killed her!"

"I don't think you understand what's involved here, Mr. Richmond," Ernie told him slowly. "You were alone on that mountain with Mrs. Richmond. You were the last one to see her alive. She was poisoned by the wine she drank and died within thirty minutes. But someone wasn't satisfied with that. Someone went out and poured honey and bear attractant on her body so no one would think to look for the poison. No one else seems to have been on the mountain. Except you!"

"It wasn't me," Donald Richmond answered. "I didn't kill Darva! It might look bad for me but it could've been one of them from the mansion. They all knew we were going up there. One of them could have put the poison into the wine then followed us up there, thinking both of us would die. Then when Darva came out and died, they decided to frame me for it."

Ernie looked skeptical.

"Did you know your wife was having an affair, Mr. Richmond?"

The man looked at Sharyn dumbfounded. All the color drained from his ruddy face. "That's a lie!"

She shook her head. "I'm afraid not. We spoke with the man this morning. He said Darva broke it off with him because she thought you were getting suspicious and she was afraid of you."

Donald's mouth worked but nothing came out for a few seconds. "There's no way! I mean, Darva wouldn't have cheated on me! We had an understanding! We were together on this! She wouldn't have been seeing anyone else!"

"Mr. Richmond—"

"That's just something those people at the mansion said to make us look bad. Darva never fooled around again. Darva loved me!"

"Again?" Sharyn asked pointedly. "Had she fooled around before, Mr. Richmond?"

There was a knock and an expensively dressed woman walked through the door. "I think you've said all you're going to say to my client, Sheriff."

"He waived his right to an attorney," Ernie informed her.

"He was under duress," she stated. "And if you try to take anything he just told you into court, I'll crucify you!"

"He was lucid and clear about what he was doing," Ernie argued.

"Mr. Richmond?" Sharyn asked him. "Is this your attorney?"

"You don't have to answer that or anything else, Donald," the lawyer told him. "My client and I would like some time alone, Sheriff. I'll decide if he has anything else he wants to tell you."

Sharyn and Ernie left them alone in the room.

Ed joined them outside the door. "I hate lawyers."

"You might not if you were on the other side of that debate," Ernie told him from experience. "Sometimes, things aren't what they seem."

"This one looks pretty open and shut to me."

Trudy brought over the arrest warrant.

"Well?" Joe asked, glancing at them as he returned.

"Did Richmond make a phone call before he sat down?" Ernie wondered.

"Nope," Joe answered. "He came along just as sweet as pie!"

"Then where did the lawyer come from?" Sharyn questioned.

Ed shrugged. "Maybe the Richmonds called her. He is kin."

The attorney came out of the room and glared at them. "You've violated my client's rights, Sheriff. I'll see you in court for this!"

"That's fine, Ms—?"

"Jill Madison-Farmer," the lawyer said, without extending her hand to Sharyn.

"You're Mike Farmer's wife!" Ernie said. "I knew you looked familiar! Mike has been my insurance agent forever."

"Well, it's too bad you couldn't have insurance for this! We'll probably end up suing your entire department!"

"In the meantime," Sharyn concluded. "We're arresting your client. He's being charged with first-degree murder." She nodded to Joe, who moved quickly into the conference room.

"That doesn't surprise me, Sheriff," Ms. Farmer said with a feline smile. "But I anticipated this move. He'll be arraigned this evening. We'll be asking for immediate release."

"On what grounds?" Ernie wondered.

Ms. Madison-Farmer shrugged her narrow shoulders in her Liz Claiborne suit. "His rights were violated. Your case is circumstantial. He didn't commit the crime. Anything else?"

"You're well prepared for a case we only just brought in," Sharyn observed. "Did you have an advance scout?"

Ms. Madison-Farmer blinked her eyes a few times, then glared at Sharyn. "Don't attempt to speak with my client again without counsel." She turned to Donald as Joe brought him out of the interrogation room. "Don't say anything else unless I'm present, Donald!"

Donald nodded blankly, then Joe led him away. Ms. Madison-Farmer smiled at them as she walked out of the office, juggling her memos and briefcase.

"How *did* she know what was going on?" Ed wondered thoughtfully, watching her walk away. "She's no accident chaser. That lady has class!"

"She's married to a friend of mine," Ernie reminded him. "I wish I'd had her when I was in trouble!"

"I don't believe the Richmond family called her in," Sharyn theorized. "I can only think of one person who might enjoy this."

"Enjoy it?" Ed asked. "Who would enjoy this?"

"Jack Winter," Ernie stated.

"Brrr!" Ed shivered. "Anybody else feel a cold draft when he said that name?"

"He's just a man," Trudy told them as she handed Sharyn her messages. "You know, Ben had a run-in with him about year ago. He wasn't so tough."

"What about?" Ed wondered.

"Some horses His Lordship owned and kept out by our place. He almost let them starve. Ben told the SPCA about it. They took the horses away from him. He had to pay a big fine and can't own a horse in this county again for three years."

"That was mighty good of Ben," Ernie acknowledged. "But it was risky. And the sheriff is in a different position. She has to work with him."

"I can handle Jack Winter," Sharyn said calmly. "Let's see what Nick has on that box of poison and the honey. Ed, run over there and wait until the results are ready. I want to know tonight, before the arraignment."

"What are you doing?" Ernie asked.

"I'm going to call Miss Eleanore and see if she has time for me. Want to come?"

Ernie nodded. "It's that 'again' thing, isn't it?"

"Yeah. Darva confided things to her. Let's see what she can tell us about the other boyfriend."

Miss Eleanore was delighted to see both of them. She had tea brought to her hotel room and asked Sharyn to pour. "Such a civilized practice."

"What can you tell us about Darva's other involvement?" Sharyn handed her a cup of tea.

"Other?" the old lady asked after a sip of the fragrant blend of mint and black tea.

"Mrs. Richmond told Tad Willis that she was involved with another man in Montana," Ernie told her gently.

"Oh, *yes!* Yes, I know who you mean now! Oh, but that was a long time ago."

"Who was it?" Sharyn asked, balancing her cup of tea on her lap.

"Well, you know Darva was an actress at a ski lodge dinner theater when she met Donald. She was a very good actress, in fact. She could have gone on to Broadway or Hollywood but she fell in love with Donald Richmond. He was demanding and unhappy. I never quite knew what she saw in him."

The old lady sat for a few moments, looking at the elaborate 'R' that graced the fine Regency Hotel china. "Oh, well, anyway." She took a fragile breath and smiled at her guests. Her brown eyes were misty. "Darva was so lovely. She attracted men to her. Donald was very jealous. They had some bad times. Darva heard from a friend of hers, a ski instructor, I believe. She was dating him before she met Donald. I suppose they could have been involved. Mind you, I'm not defending her but she was very unhappy."

"Of course." Sharyn tried to understand without judging the dead woman. "What happened to the ski instructor?"

Eleanore looked confused. "I'm not quite sure. I saw him a few times. I remember she told me Donald wouldn't even let her talk to him. I was afraid for her. I guess the man just left or whatever."

Sharyn considered her next question carefully before putting it to the woman. "Darva told her new lover here that Donald killed her lover in Montana. Did she ever say anything like that to you?"

"Oh, no! I'm sure he must be mistaken!" She shook her head, the silver-white ringlets dancing around her face.

"Do you recall the name of the ski instructor, ma'am?" Ernie asked her. "So we could look him up."

"Let me see." Eleanore puzzled for a few moments. "It was . . . his face is so clear in my mind! I just can't think . . . oh yes! Jack—no, John. John Jackson! That's it! He was a handsome man!"

"Thank you, Miz Eleanore," Ernie said, writing down the man's name in his notebook.

"Do you have to leave so soon?" she asked sweetly.

"I'm afraid so, but you've been a big help," Sharyn told her with a smile. "How long are you staying in town?"

"Just until my niece is properly laid to rest. I want to make sure the thing is done right."

"I understand," Sharyn agreed. "I'll let you know if we hear anything else about her death."

"Thank you, Sheriff." Miss Eleanore held out a hand encased in a white glove. It trembled just slightly when Sharyn took it but the old lady's grip was firm.

"Thank you . . . uh—uh—" Sharyn started sneezing. She was too close to the rose perfume.

"You should be home in bed with some soup, Sheriff!" Miss Eleanore said with a nod.

"I—I . . ." She sneezed again. She waved her hand to the woman and left the room.

"Roses again, huh?" Ernie asked as he joined her.

"It's her perfume or whatever," Sharyn explained, sniffling. "I expect it at dinners and public places because of the roses on the tables. I usually don't have this problem with individuals."

They got out of the elevator just in time to see Faye Howard at the concierge's desk.

"Ernie! Sharyn! I'm so glad to see you!"

"Mom," Sharyn said with a sniff.

"Sharyn, your face is all blotchy!" her mother declared. "What have you been doing?"

Sharyn shook her head. "Roses. I'm going to the rest room for a minute."

"Good! When you come back, you can help me look at the plans for the ballroom. I'm so excited about the party!"

"All right." Sharyn sniffed and looked at Ernie through watery eyes. "You might as well take the car and head

home, Ernie. There's nothing else you have to do tonight.
Go home to Annie. Mom can drop me off at the office. I'll
call you when the arraignment is over."

"You sure about that?" he asked. "I can stay."

"I'm glad to have you back," she said with a smile.
"Let's get you home at a decent hour whenever we can,
huh?"

Ernie smiled. "Thanks, Sheriff. You'll call if you need
me?"

"I will. Now go home!"

Ernie waited until Sharyn disappeared into the women's
bathroom, then he took Faye Howard by the arm. "You and
me are gonna have a little talk, Faye."

"What about, Ernie? Where are we going?"

"Let's stroll towards the ballroom. You can say you were
showing me the party plans, if Sharyn asks."

"Ernie?" Faye said, seeing the grim look on his face. "Is
something wrong?"

"Nothing that can't be corrected, Faye. I'm only gonna
say this to you because T. Raymond isn't here to say it and
I know he'd want me to say it in his place."

Sharyn came out of the bathroom and took a deep breath
before she went to meet her mother in the ballroom. Her
eyes were puffy but she'd stopped sneezing. She caught
sight of Ernie as he was walking out the big front doors.

"Mom?" she called out as she walked into the ballroom.

Her mother was at the other end of the room, staring out
the window at the lights in the street that led down to the
lake. "There must be a play going on across the street,"
Faye said. "A popular one by the number of people there
tonight."

"Maybe."

Faye sat down on one of the graceful, gilded chairs and

patted the one beside her for her daughter to sit down. "Please, Sharyn, sit by me."

Sharyn sat beside her mother. She wondered what she'd done to warrant this attention.

"Sharyn, you and I have never been very alike," Faye began. "You've always been more like your father. Stubborn. Independent. Strong. I'm not made that way."

Sharyn looked at her mother's pretty face. She looked like she'd been crying. "What's wrong, Mom?"

Faye took her daughter's hand. "I love you, Sharyn. You know that, don't you? I know your father and you were close. I know we could never have a relationship like that but I will always love you. I want the best for you."

"I know that," Sharyn puzzled. "I love you, too, Mom."

Faye smiled at Sharyn and touched her hand to her bright red curls. "Caison is like you and your father. I suppose that's why you don't get along. But it's why we *do* get along. Do you understand? I need someone like that in my life again."

"I understand," Sharyn acknowledged carefully. "I don't trust Caison but I know you've known him a lot longer than me. If he's right for you, I think you should marry him."

"Do you really?" Faye asked. "I would feel so much better if I knew you felt that way."

"I do, Mom," Sharyn assured her. "Maybe part of me is a little jealous that he's taking you away from me."

"He couldn't take me away from you, honey! I'm your mother. I know we have our differences. It's been pointed out to me that, sometimes, I might make too much of those differences. Maybe I'm a little hard on you. But I only want what's best for you."

"I know, Mom."

"Then you'll understand why I'm going to say what I'm going to say. Promise me that you'll think about it."

Sharyn swallowed hard. *Here it comes.* "Okay."

"Ever since you took this job, a part of me screams every time you walk out the door. I can't face the idea that some-day, you could be on the floor like your father, riddled with bullets. You've had your share of close calls already." She picked up both of Sharyn's hands. "Give this up, Sharyn. Take the bar. Do what you set out to do before your father was killed. You didn't plan this life for yourself. It just happened to you. Don't you think I could see the horror and grief on your face? I'm begging you, don't run for re-election next year."

"Mom, I—"

"You promised you'd think about it," Faye reminded her, kissing her hands. "I just want you to be happy and alive. If you decide to go on in the job, I'll support you. But my soul will shriek in pain when they announce that you're the winner again."

Sharyn stared at her mother. "Are you saying our prob-lems are caused by me being sheriff?"

"No, of course not," Faye replied. "It would just make me feel better to know you won't run again."

"Mom." Sharyn stood up and paced the red carpet. "I don't understand. This is like asking you to give up mar-rying Caison!"

"This wasn't your dream job," Faye said harshly. "You felt obligated—"

"I like what I do!"

"Are you saying you'll give up the job if I give up Cai-son?"

"No." Sharyn shook her head. "I don't want you to give up Caison if you want to be with him."

Faye nodded. "Good. I just want you to think about this. Don't make a decision right now. I promise things are go-ing to change between us, Sharyn. You'll see."

Night court was at eight-thirty. Sharyn stayed in the ballroom and listened to her mother explain about gold lamé hanging in ripples from the ceiling. The flowers would be gold mums and asters, in deference to Sharyn's allergy to roses. There would be golden place cards and tiny golden harps that were made into baskets to hold them for each guest.

"I'd like you to wear gold, too, Sharyn," her mother said. "Kristie will be wearing gold and so will I. Fortunately, it compliments all three of us."

The orchestra would be playing love songs and a shower of golden balloons would be released when the engagement was formally announced. Two doves would also be released from the rooftop. The drink would be golden champagne.

"The golden theme will be in keeping with our golden future together," Faye explained, taking in a quick breath. "What do you think?"

"It sounds elegant," Sharyn said, finding a word that would suit her mother.

"Oh, it will be. It will be the biggest event of the social season! I don't have the menu yet but the Regency chef is working on something special for me."

Sharyn glanced at her watch. "It'll be wonderful, Mom." She hugged her mother carefully, mindful of her hair and make-up. "I'm sure you and the Senator will be very happy together."

"I know we will, Sharyn! You could come to the capital to live with us. Just think of the splendid opportunities there would be for you there as a lawyer! And the eligible men!"

"I have to go," Sharyn said on that note. "I have to be at an arraignment in a few minutes. Let me know if there's anything I can do."

Faye smiled and pressed her hands to her heart. "You could make your announcement not to run for sheriff again during the party."

Sharyn smiled. *No pressure there!* "I'm thinking about what you said, Mom. That's all I can promise you."

"Thank you, honey! You know how much it means to me! Didn't you need me to drop you at the courthouse?"

"No. I'll walk," Sharyn answered with a smile. "It's a nice night." Sharyn left her mother in the ballroom with her dreams of golden lamé and golden champagne.

The playhouse across the street was well lit. Sounds of music and laughter drifted across the street to her from its old halls. The play was already in progress so not many people lingered on the street. With nightfall came a cold breeze from Diamond Lake. The sun had made the day seem warmer than it was but the night was chilly. Sharyn buttoned up her jacket and put her hands into her pockets.

She could see the top of Diamond Mountain from there. There was a small flashing red light that alerted planes to its dark hulk. The rest of the Uwharries were dark shapes around it. They looked like smooth, black outlines without the daylight. No trees. No dangerous trails. No man-eating bears.

Sharyn knew that was what her mother wanted for her. That was the 'best', she supposed. A smooth, calm life without any dangers and a husband who would give her the life her mother thought she deserved.

Faye was right about one thing. Sharyn hadn't planned on being the sheriff of Diamond Springs. She'd planned on being a lawyer and defending people accused of crimes they didn't commit. She'd always planned on coming back to Diamond Springs and having lunch with her father a few times a week where they could debate who was guilty and who was innocent. T. Raymond Howard was the sheriff of Diamond Springs. Not Sharyn Howard.

Did that mean there was something wrong with her being the sheriff? Maybe she wasn't following her original plan but things had changed. Her father was dead. She'd helped bring in his killers because she was the sheriff. If she'd been a defense attorney, she might have had to defend them. Her legal background came in handy to her in her job.

But hadn't she always thought the job should have been Ernie's? He'd been her father's right-hand man, as he was hers. He had deserved the position from seniority and experience. But he had refused to run when T. Raymond was killed. Sharyn thought she understood why now. Rather than Ernie's explanation about not wanting to deal with the politics, she felt pretty sure he hadn't wanted his secret about the old training school to get out. Of course, being sheriff would only make things harder for him and Annie.

Sharyn felt like she did a good job as sheriff. The question, she thought as she put her hand on the courthouse door, was whether it was the way she wanted to spend her life. She opened the door and a bevy of reporters, including Foster Odom, caught sight of her.

"Sheriff!" he yelled over the crowd. "Is there a reason you're prosecuting the Richmond family?"

Chapter Seven

"Who's the judge?" Sharyn asked Ed when she joined him in the courtroom. She'd evaded most of the reporters' questions about the Richmond murder and arrest.

"The Honorable Tim Dailey," Ed told her quietly. "How lucky was that?"

Joe joined them there, with a nod of his dark head. "Well, Judge White was supposed to preside over the court tonight. Last-minute substitution."

"Judge White?" Sharyn frowned. "No-bail White replaced by a friend of the Richmond family?"

Joe shrugged and watched the proceedings. Their prisoner sat in front of them with his attorney.

"Ed? Anything on that box of poison or the jar?"

"Nothing on the poison itself yet," Ed told her. "Everyone else in the house, except for Darva and Donald, had their prints on the box. The honey jar was clean. And the piece of material was a scrap that was torn from the hem of Mrs. Richmond's robe. I don't think the bear did that."

"I'll be back," Sharyn said, getting up to move behind

the ADA. She spoke briefly with the young man who looked uncomfortable in his brown suit and brown tie. "You need to challenge this judge."

"Challenge the judge?" the young man wondered. "I've only been in this job three days! How can I challenge the judge?"

"He's biased, a friend of the Richmond family. If you let him stay—"

"All rise. The Honorable Judge Tim Dailey presiding over Circuit Court 813."

"All right," Judge Dailey began, glancing through the papers on his desk. "Let's get through this with the minimum of fuss, shall we? Is the State ready?"

"Yes, Your Honor," the young ADA got to his feet like a puppet jerked by a string.

"And the defense?"

"Yes, Your Honor," Ms. Madison-Farmer proclaimed. "And I'd like to ask now that these charges be thrown out of court."

"I don't do that here, Counselor," Judge Dailey told her. "But I'll take that as an innocent plea from your client?"

"Yes, Your Honor," the lawyer spoke up. Donald nodded.

"Bail?"

"The State requests that the defendant be held without bail, Your Honor, because he is a flight risk and has plenty of resources."

"Defense?"

"Your Honor, the man has family here in Diamond Springs. He was born and raised here even though he hasn't lived here for a long time. His wife is going to be buried here. I don't think he's going to leave before she's properly taken care of."

Judge Dailey glanced at the paperwork again. "I can't

agree to no bail on a murder charge but I can see the defense attorney's point. Bail is set at fifty thousand dollars."

Sharyn shot to her feet. "Fifty thousand? Your Honor, with all due respect, a man was given more bail last week for running his tractor into his neighbor's house!"

There were a few hints of laughter among the reporters in the courtroom.

"Order!" The judge pounded his gavel. "You're out of line, Sheriff Howard! Sit down!"

"Your Honor, if the ADA could have a moment in your chambers to explain why you shouldn't be involved in this case at all for personal bias—"

"I said, sit down, Sheriff Howard, or you're going to find yourself sharing a cell with your prisoner!"

The ADA glanced at Sharyn and shook his head, not daring to look at the stern-faced judge.

"I've made my ruling. Bail is set at fifty thousand." He banged his gavel. "Next case!"

Sharyn walked right up to the bench, oblivious to the hand movements and head shaking from her deputies. "Judge Dailey, you don't want to do this!"

"Sheriff Howard—"

"Don't you think everyone knows? Don't you think those reporters are going to report that you were soft on Donald Richmond because you were his brother's friend?"

"Sheriff—"

"I object to the Sheriff questioning the judge," Ms. Madison-Farmer said loudly while the buzz in the courtroom behind Sharyn increased.

Judge Dailey banged his gavel down again. His face was red with anger. "Bailiff, take the Sheriff to the holding cell for contempt! I warned you, Sheriff! You can't be involved with this procedure! If the ADA isn't complaining, why are you up here?"

"You know you shouldn't be involved with this," she repeated.

"Bailiff!"

The bailiff was a head shorter than Sharyn. He took her arm and told her to come along quietly. Ed and Joe shook their heads and approached the ADA, who looked lost and bewildered. They spoke in hurried sentences and glanced at Sharyn, who was being led away to a holding cell. The press scrambled from the courtroom. There was no way to actually photograph Sharyn being led away. There was a wall between them and the holding area where prisoners waited before being transferred to the county jail. But they could speculate.

Sharyn sat in a cell next to Donald for a while. It didn't take long, however, before someone came to post bail for him. She heard Ed and Joe arguing with the guard standing outside the holding area. They were demanding to see her, demanding her release. Sharyn was contemplating her mother's words. Maybe she shouldn't be the sheriff.

There was only one person in Diamond Springs who could have fingers long enough to reach out and touch this case. For whatever reason, Jack Winter had decided to intervene. He had sent in a rookie ADA on a murder hearing. Somehow, he'd manipulated the judge to get the right person to set the lowest bail possible. And she believed that he might have played both sides by sending Jill Madison-Farmer to represent Donald Richmond.

Just as she had convinced herself that she was overestimating the man and allowing all the stories of his dark and nefarious deeds to sway her, the young ADA from the courtroom came for her. "If you could come with me, Sheriff."

"Where?" she asked without rising.

"Mr. Winter would like a word with you. Then you're free to go."

She smiled. Maybe her father and Ernie were right about the DA. "What about the judge?"

"Mr. Winter spoke with Judge Dailey on your behalf."

"So I'm free to go right now?"

"Yes, ma'am." The young man gulped so hard, Sharyn could hear him swallow.

"That's fine," she finished. "I'd like a word with Mr. Winter myself."

They handed her gun to her at the back door out of the courthouse. The ADA took her up a back set of stairs that led directly to the DA's office on the top floor of the pink granite building. The press was still waiting in the street and on the sidewalk just outside the courthouse.

Lennie wasn't around when they reached the big office. The young ADA vanished as soon as they arrived.

"Come in, Sharyn," Jack Winter called from the inner office where she could hear the strains of Mozart.

Sharyn followed the sound. There was a small table set for two. He was lighting a candle in the middle of the fresh flowers that graced it.

"I heard about your allergy to roses," he said smoothly. "Pansies." He pointed out the yellow and purple flowers. "I hope you're hungry. I haven't eaten all day myself. I had Lennie go out for some Chinese for us. I hope you like Mandarin?"

"Is that all Lennie is here? A glorified errand boy?"

Jack smiled at her. "No. He's learning the ropes. When he's ready, he'll be my new ADA."

"In place of the kid in court tonight?"

"Yes."

"What will happen to him?"

Jack smiled. "Perhaps you could make him one of your deputies?"

"Why?" she asked. "What did you hope to gain by helping Richmond?"

"I wasn't helping Donald Richmond," he told her. "I was making a point with you."

"What?"

"Come and sit down, Sharyn! Don't be so fussy and intense. You'll live longer!"

Sharyn took a deep breath. "What was the point?"

He glanced at her, his pale eyes appreciating her features but not moving beyond her face. "I have a proposition for you."

"For me?"

"Sit down, Sharyn!" He smiled. "Please."

Sharyn sat down on the edge of the chair as though anything else might contaminate her uniform. "All right."

"You're a great deal like your father. But you're better. Smarter." He sat down at the table across from her. "I want you to come and work for me. I know you're only the bar away from your law degree. Forget Lennie. Be my new ADA."

"I already have a job."

"A job that doesn't appreciate you or your talents. I would appreciate both you . . . and your talents. And I would reward them both handsomely."

"If I wanted to be a lawyer, I'd be one," she charged.

"I know you wanted to fill in for your father," he said carefully. "And you've done an admirable job. Now let one of those rash young men take over. I need you here, beside me."

Sharyn studied his too smooth, too perfect features. His soft voice curled around her spine and permeated her brain. The man was smart and charismatic. It was a struggle just to look away from him. There was a hypnotic quality to his voice and his eyes. Her hands were icy and her face was hot. She could feel him impelling her to agree with him, give in to his iron will.

Then she touched her grandfather's service revolver and

her brain cleared. She was repulsed by being in the same room with him. "Thank you for the offer. I'm sure it's a generous one. But I'm happy being the sheriff."

"Pity."

She leaned towards him. "Don't forget again that I *am* the sheriff here, Mr. Winter. You almost confessed to tampering with the legal system tonight. I don't have to witness the crime to take in the perpetrator."

Jack smiled. His hand caressed his wine glass. "Do you really think there would be any proof, Sharyn? I've had this position since before your father became sheriff."

"Did you make him the same offer?"

"No. I didn't have the same . . . fancy . . . for him that I have for you."

Sharyn got to her feet. "I appreciate your interest, sir. You and I are on the same team for now. Let's keep it that way." She turned to leave him.

"You're very young, Sharyn," he said to her. "And very naive. There's a power behind every town. People like me and Caison Talbot and Beau Richmond. We make the decisions. We decide who is going to play. And who isn't going to be re-elected."

Sharyn walked back to where he sat, outlined by the glow from the candle in the dark room. "Beau Richmond is dead, Mr. Winter."

"So is your father, Sharyn."

She felt like he had stabbed her. She didn't let it show. "I have to work with you. But I don't have to like you. And if I catch even the slightest hint of impropriety from this office again—"

The District Attorney laughed. "Has Nick told you yet how delightful you look when you're angry?"

Sharyn stalked out of his office. The young ADA entered as soon as he saw her leave the room. "Is there anything else I can do for you tonight, sir?"

"Get out of here, you idiot!" The DA threw a glass at the younger man. It barely missed his head. When he was gone and Jack Winter's anger at being challenged by that *girl* had lessened, he dialed Caison Talbot's phone number.

Ed, Joe, and Nick were waiting in front of the courthouse for her.

"Where have you been, Sheriff?" Ed asked, relieved to see her. "They said they let you go almost an hour ago!"

Sharyn glanced back at the light still shining in the DA's office. "Talking to our esteemed district attorney."

"What did he say?" Joe wondered.

"I should've known he was behind all of this!" Ed shook his head.

"What were you doing up there for that long with him?" Nick demanded.

"He offered me a job." She related some of the experience to them.

"He wants you to give up being sheriff! If that don't beat all!" Ed remarked.

"He asked your daddy the same thing once," Joe told her. "Offered him a job as the mayor. Said he'd sponsor him to run for office and see that he won."

"Now you see why we told you not to mess with him?" Ed considered. "He's a bad one, Sheriff."

"He all but told me that he set this whole thing up tonight," she informed them. "Maybe I'm wrong but I think that's against the law."

"You'd never be able to prove it," Ed promised her. "He's as smart and as quick as an old 'possum!"

"Even 'possums can be trapped, Ed!" She smiled at the analogy. "Anyone else up for a cup of coffee!"

Ed looked at Joe, who shook his head when he glanced at Nick's dark face. They made their excuses quickly.

Sharyn and Nick were left standing on the street corner. She looked at him.

"Coffee?" he suggested.

"Yes." She shivered as the cold breeze jostled the new leaves that were left on the trees.

"Come on," he urged. "It's too cold to stand out here talking about it."

With her hand around a hot mug of mocha with sprinkles, Sharyn felt something inside of her finally relax. Her shoulders slumped a little. She was exhausted.

"Tired?" Nick asked.

"Yes," she replied. "It's been a long day."

"And you didn't expect to end up in jail?"

"Holding," she corrected. "I wasn't arrested for anything."

He swallowed a sip of hot coffee, without sprinkles. "Okay. Holding. A little cell *before* they take you to the county jail."

"Your point?"

"You can't fight Winter."

"Not you, too," she complained.

"Not up front anyway," he continued. "You're an honest person, Sharyn. Surely you've noticed that not everyone is like you?"

"And?"

"You have to fight Winter the way he fights. Sneaky and underhanded. He's been the scum behind so much in this town for so long that it's no wonder Ed and Joe think you can't win against him."

She stared at him. "But you think I could win?"

He nodded. "Only if you don't give him the chance to beat you. You can't think any of the people he owns will turn against him."

"But why did he do this with Donald Richmond?" she questioned. "Old times' sake?"

"Not on your life! He was trying to put you in your place. He showed you what he can do."

"Okay." She considered his words. "I have to sort out this Richmond thing before I can tackle Jack Winter."

"What's to sort out?"

She shrugged. "Something isn't right."

He groaned.

"It hasn't felt right from the beginning."

"Not the gut instinct again!"

She realized what he was saying. "Are you saying I'm wrong?"

"No," he responded with a grin. "I'm saying your gut instinct always means more work for me and all of the theories I've worked hard to prove so far are out the window."

"I don't know that for sure."

"But gut instinct is telling you that, huh?"

She nodded, then was silent for a long moment. "Winter mentioned that he and Caison Talbot and Beau Richmond run this town. I told him that Beau Richmond was dead." She looked up at Nick. "He told me that my father was dead, too. It was the *way* he said it."

Nick covered her hand with his and wished he could just go to his car and take out several of his guns and solve the problem for her.

"My mother is marrying into this, Nick."

"You could tell her," he added.

"She'd never believe me. She'd think it was just something else to make trouble for her and Caison."

"You have been fairly vocal about the senator," he answered.

Sharyn looked at his hand covering hers. He had long, narrow fingers and his touch was warm. "I'm sorry about this afternoon."

He moved his hand and swallowed the rest of his coffee.

"Don't be. You were right. We do work together. I've gone to parties before with co-workers. It's okay."

"Nick—"

"Really, Sharyn. It's okay." He said the words but he couldn't look at her when he said them.

She glanced at her watch. It was past midnight. "I should go home. We should both go home and get some sleep. Tomorrow might be another tough day."

"Especially with your gut instinct working overtime?"

"Yeah. Thanks for listening."

"Hey, what are co-workers for?"

"And friends, I hope," she said, holding out her hand to him.

He looked at her hand then took it in his, his fingers sliding across hers. "Friends. Of course."

"I would like to go with you to the engagement party," she told him, not letting go of his hand. "If you don't, I mean, I know you could probably find someone else who would be—"

He squeezed her hand gently. "I would love to take you to your mother's engagement party, Sharyn. There isn't anyone I'd like to take more."

Later that night in her bed, Sharyn thought about Nick's words. She touched her hand and still felt the warmth of his grip. It was good that she and Nick were friends. It was good that they worked so well together. He was clever and good at what he did. He was handsome and well spoken and tall. She had always had a problem being taller than the men she dated.

Not that she was dating Nick, she reminded herself in a panic. Only that if she *were* dating him, he would be taller than her, even in heels. He could be sarcastic and moody, as dark as his eyes when something wasn't going his way. He was stubborn and opinionated and he carried an arsenal of guns in his car that he protected like it was his child.

She could never see herself dating someone like Nick. She smiled and went to sleep, her hand still tingling from his touch.

The next day was overcast and felt like snow. Kristie was home, crunching cereal for breakfast while her mother ate grits. The television was on in the kitchen.

Sharyn walked into the kitchen in her slippers and robe, thinking that for just a brief moment, it could have been three years ago. Kristie was still in high school. Her father was still alive and watching the news on television before he went to work. Her mother would be trying to iron his shirt or get him to eat something besides Pop Tarts for breakfast. They were still a family.

"Hi Sharyn," Kristie said, looking up. "Want some fruity flakes?"

"No thanks," Sharyn grimaced, propelled back into the present day.

"You know Sharyn doesn't eat breakfast, dear," Faye told her younger daughter.

"Shhh!" Kristie said suddenly. "Look! There's Sharyn!"

". . . in what's seen as a setback for the sheriff's department in the Darva Richmond murder case, Sheriff Sharyn Howard was charged with contempt in the arraignment proceedings and held for several hours after the hearing."

"Sharyn!" Faye said in a shocked voice.

"It wasn't several hours," Sharyn responded. "Only about two hours."

"Wow! Were you really in jail?" Kristie asked.

"No," Sharyn retorted sharply. "Just in holding."

". . . Donald Richmond was held on fifty thousand dollars' bond but was released late last night." The commentary had pictures of Donald leaving the jail with another old friend of Beau Richmond's, ex-district court judge, Walter Hamilton.

"So that's who bailed him out!"

"Doesn't Walter look polished in his suit and tie?" her mother added. "I'm so used to seeing him in his black robe."

"Until we all found out that he was involved in that last murder," Kristie said with a wide smile. "Oops! Have to go! I'm meeting Keith and we're going to visit his folks out in Bell's Creek today."

"Bell's Creek?" Faye mused over her cup of sassafras tea. "I haven't heard that name since they shut down the campground out there."

"Keith's father is the pastor at the church out there," Kristie explained. "We're gonna go walk through the spooky old campground."

"Well, be careful," her mother said. "That place must be ready to fall apart."

"It's been there a hundred years or so, hasn't it?" Sharyn asked.

"At least," Faye replied. "Some dreadful things happened out there."

"Ooooo," Kristie said with a laugh. "You didn't tell me that you know ghost stories about the place?"

"I don't. And there are no ghosts! Don't we get enough of that around here from tourists looking for the 'ghosts' of the Uwharries?"

Sharyn laughed. "Just be careful, Kristie. Those old buildings can be death traps."

"I will be," her sister said. "You two are both such worriers! I can understand Mom. But you're not that old yet, Sharyn!"

"I'm not that old either!" Faye objected.

Kristie laughed and kissed her mother. "Bye!"

"When she's not building houses for poor people in Arkansas, she's traipsing through deserted buildings here! Why hasn't that been torn down yet, Sharyn?"

Sharyn swallowed her juice in a gulp. "Why are you asking me?"

"You *are* the sheriff of this county. You do have some influence."

"Not over private property, unless it's an eyesore. Bell's Creek is so far out in the county, I doubt that anybody thinks about the campground anymore."

"Well, you should think about it," Faye said shortly, "Have you looked for a gold dress yet?"

"Not yet," Sharyn told her. "I'm in the middle of a murder investigation. But I'll have one in time for the party."

Faye smiled. "That's good."

The dark sky was heavy with snow when Sharyn left the house. The weather report was calling for snow and ice that night. If they got it, it would mean pulling a double shift while Diamond Springs tried to keep from panicking and dug out. Her cell phone was quiet for a change, which she attributed to changing her number. She talked to Josh Hartsell, their part-time psychologist, about his interview with Donald Richmond. Nothing he said surprised her.

There were a few stray reporters at the back gate when she reached the office but Charlie waved her into the parking lot while he pushed them aside.

Ernie met her at the back door, bristling with information. "I did a quick check into that old boyfriend of Darva's that Miss Eleanore told us about yesterday." He handed her a printout of a newspaper article. "The editor at the paper in Montana sent me this. John Jackson *is* dead."

Sharyn took off her coat and scarf as she read the article and walked into the office.

"Emergency teams are standing by in case of snow tonight, Sheriff," Trudy told her.

"Thanks, Trudy."

"Good morning, Sheriff Howard," JP said with a wide smile on his face.

"Good morning, JP. How's nights?"

"Fine, Sheriff Howard. Not so exciting as the day shift but I kept busy."

"Good," Sharyn said with a smile for him in return. "Are you and David getting along?"

JP shrugged. "Is David supposed to be working the nights with me?"

Joe heard his nephew's name. "Don't bother!" he told Sharyn. "Let me!"

Sharyn patted JP on the shoulder. "We might be having snow tonight so go home and get as much sleep as you can. Sometimes we all have to work for twenty-four hours straight if the weather turns bad."

JP nodded. "I will go home right away and sleep. Please call me if you need my help."

"Thanks. I will."

Ernie followed Sharyn towards the conference room. "Trudy, give Nick a call for me."

"No point," Trudy said as Nick opened the door to the room. "He's been here for a few minutes already. Eleanore Lacey wants to talk to you again, Sheriff."

"Thanks," Sharyn replied. "Good morning, Nick. Hold my calls, Trudy."

Ed joined them in the conference room. His good-looking face was red with cold but he was smiling as he took off his jacket. "Sarah called Joe last night. They're having dinner together."

"Great," Sharyn said. "I hope they get back together."

"Me, too! If I have to listen to him whine once more about me leaving the cap off the toothpaste—"

Sharyn agreed about the whining. "I know what you mean. Joe is going to sort out something with David but I'd like to see what we can come up with on this Richmond murder."

"What's the problem? Seems to me we have enough evidence to convict him," Ed said, taking a seat.

"Sharyn's gut is bothering her," Nick told them.

Ed groaned. "Can't this be the time that everything is just working the way it should?"

After frowning at Nick, Sharyn showed them the copy of the newspaper. "This is the man Eleanore Lacey told us about."

"He skied into a tree!" Ed said quickly. "I don't think anyone could call that murder!"

"Nick, I'd appreciate it if you would call the ME in Elkton and get the full report. Ernie is going to check into Darva's background with the man."

"And what are we hoping to accomplish?"

"Donald Richmond's fingerprints weren't on that box of poison," she told Ed.

"And I got the results back this morning," Nick told them. "That was the box the poison came from."

"He could've worn gloves," Ernie suggested.

Sharyn took a deep breath. "He didn't have a motive to kill his wife."

"She was sleeping with that weird artist guy down at the train depot," Ed reminded her. "That could be motive."

"He definitely had opportunity," Ernie added.

"I'd be willing to bet that Donald didn't know Darva was sleeping with anyone. None of the family at the mansion knew she was having an affair. They heard them argue about leaving and not claiming the money but that was all. Donald said the same thing when he was here. He was shocked that Darva was seeing another man, wasn't he, Ernie?"

Ernie shrugged. "Or he's a good actor. There's still the jar of honey and the piece of the robe."

Sharyn turned to him. "Ernie, do you think Donald killed his wife?"

"The whole thing about somebody else from the mansion sneaking out to the mountain and killing her sounds kind of far-fetched," he replied. "Other than that, I guess I didn't feel like he killed Mrs. Richmond."

"All right," Sharyn began again.

"Unless he's a psycho," Ernie continued.

"I talked to Josh Hartsell on my way in this morning," Sharyn told them. "He interviewed Donald with Ms. Madison-Farmer's permission, and he told me that he doesn't think the man has a psychotic personality. He also doesn't see him as being the kind of person who could plan a crime like this."

Nick looked at Ed and Ernie. "I think you're grasping at straws, Sharyn."

"Some people are just guilty, Sheriff," Ed added to it.

"I know," she assured them both, "but humor me. If we look into all of these other aspects and still come up with the same answers, I'll let it go. Okay?"

"You're the sheriff," Ed replied.

"Yes, ma'am," Ernie agreed.

"What am I doing again?" Nick questioned.

Sharyn glared at him and he picked up his notebook. "Ernie, check into John Jackson for me. Find out whatever you can about him, including any links to Darva or Donald. Ed, give Joe a call and have him meet you at the mansion when he's done with his problem."

"You mean David?"

"Yes, David. I'm going to call for a search warrant for Darva and Donald's rooms at the mansion. Pick it up on your way out and see what you can find."

"What are we looking for, Sheriff?"

"Anything out of the ordinary. I want to know when they got here and something more about their lives in Montana. Check out their assets. Donald said they would've been okay without the Richmond money. Check for anything that might have given away that Darva was having an affair."

"Okay, Sheriff. I'll call Joe."

"Thanks. Nick—"

"I know," he replied. "Check out the dead guy and how he got to be that way."

"Thanks! Any questions?" No one said anything. "Great. Let me know as soon as any of you have anything."

"You going to see Miz Eleanore again?" Ernie wondered.

"I think so. Will you try to find out when Darva's funeral is, Ernie?"

"Yes, ma'am."

"Thanks."

Sharyn decided to drive to The Regency Hotel. It was cold and she didn't trust the unpredictability of the weather. It could start snowing or freezing rain could pelt them. The sky was threatening and ominous, the darkest clouds skimming down over Diamond Mountain. She hoped Kristie was watching the weather, too. She would hate for her to be stranded out in the country. It could take two or three days for the plows to reach her.

She parked in the parking deck below the hotel that had been added as an afterthought just a few years ago. She went up the elevator to Room 307 and Miss Eleanore called for her to come in.

Sharyn took a step into the room and was hit immediately by the scent of roses. It was overpowering, suffocating, in the hot room. She looked up and the room was full of roses. All colors and all sizes graced the tables. There were three bottles of essential rose oil on one of the small tables. Her eyes were watering and she started sneezing before she'd taken a step into the room.

"Miss Eleanore," she spoke to the woman.

"Sheriff Howard."

She sneezed hard a few times. "I—uh—have a problem with roses. Could we go into another room to talk?"

"Oh, my poor legs bother me so on cold days like this, Sheriff. You understand. But I'll be brief." She took out a piece of paper. "I received this yesterday. It was forwarded from my home address."

Sharyn looked at the document. There was no envelope. It was a letter from an insurance company. It said simply that her niece had died and that her life insurance would be paid to her husband. "Why was this sent to you, ma'am?" Sharyn asked, taking a tissue from the old woman and wiping her streaming eyes.

"I'm the executrix of Darva's estate, of course. She wouldn't have trusted Donald! Look at that date, Sheriff! And look at that amount!"

Sharyn could barely see the letter but she wiped her eyes and held her nose to keep from sneezing. The policy was for five million dollars.

"The date is the same day that Donald found out that his brother had left him nothing in his will. You see, Sheriff! He had it all planned!"

Chapter Eight

Sharyn's cell phone went off. She sniffed and blew her nose again, then sneezed a few more times. "I'll check this out, Miss Eleanore, thanks."

"You do have a terrible time with these flowers, Sheriff. My mother always said a good cure for an allergy was to be around it as much as you could, and drink hot peppermint tea with honey."

"Thank you, Miss Eleanore," Sharyn replied, anxious to get out of that room. "I'll let you know what I find out."

Sharyn left the old lady, glad to be out of the room. She answered her cell phone in the elevator. "Yes?"

"Sheriff?" Ernie wondered.

"It's me, Ernie." She sniffed and snorted. "Miss Eleanore loves roses."

"I've got some bad news," he continued. "Ed and Joe responded to a call a few minutes ago. It was Donald Richmond. They've taken him to the hospital with a bullet in his brain. Joe said it doesn't look good."

"Suicide?"

"Joe thought it looked like it but he didn't see a note."

"Did they find him at the mansion?"

"No, some hotel off of Eighth Street, by the old bridge."

"Have them tape it off, Ernie," she said. "Don't let anyone in or out and call Nick."

"Meet you at the hospital?"

"Yeah," she answered, trying to stifle a sneeze and failing. "I'll see you there."

Sharyn opened her window and put the blue light on the top of her Jeep. She left it open, grateful for the cool, clean breeze blowing in her face. It helped blow some of the rose scent out of her sinuses and she stopped sneezing. She could still feel the congestion in her head. She hoped she could function normally when she reached the hospital. They might only have a few seconds with Donald Richmond to find out what happened. She didn't want to be sneezing her way through it.

It was too early in the year to start allergy shots and she couldn't drive taking over-the-counter medication for her allergies. She was probably going to have to grit her teeth and hope she didn't have many other interviews with Eleanore Lacey. Her perfume had been bad enough but the roses in the hot room were awful. The old lady had been helpful, though. The insurance was the clincher. Sharyn couldn't argue in Donald's defense any longer. Gut instinct might tell her that he was innocent but maybe the rose allergy had made that unreliable.

She swung into the hospital parking lot and parked close to the door at the emergency room. Ernie saw her as he parked and they ran into the emergency room together.

"Donald Richmond," Sharyn said a little breathlessly from the run and the roses.

The nurse looked at her blankly. "You kin?'

"No." Sharyn flashed her badge. "I'm the sheriff."

The nurse looked even more dubious. "You couldn't see

him even if you were kin but you have less of a chance as a cop!"

Sharyn held the other woman's eyes. "I'm not a cop. I'm the sheriff of this county. Donald Richmond is a suspect in a murder investigation. If there's any chance we could talk to him, we need to have it."

"I'll ask the doctor," the nurse told her slowly.

"Sheriff!" Ernie called, waving her back to one of the emergency rooms.

"Never mind," Sharyn told the other woman. "I'll ask him. Thanks."

Sharyn walked back to where Ernie was looking in the window at one of the closed rooms. "Let's go," she decided, pushing open the door.

"What are you doing in here?" the head nurse asked. "You can't just walk in here and—"

"I'm the sheriff and this man is a suspect in a murder investigation," Sharyn repeated. "If there's any chance we could get a statement from him—"

"There's no chance," the doctor told her. "He *was* the suspect in a murder investigation. I guess he didn't like the odds."

Ernie shook his head.

"Time of death, eleven-forty," the doctor told the nurse. "Cause of death, gunshot wound to the head."

"Could I see him, please?" Sharyn asked quietly.

The doctor shrugged. "I guess so."

She walked to the form under the green sheet on the table. With a deliberate hand, she pulled back the sheet and looked at Donald Richmond's face.

"Gunshot was to the back and side of the head," the doctor explained to her. "The bullet lodged in his brain and did massive damage. Even if we could have revived him, he would have been a mushroom."

"There will have to be an autopsy on this," she said to

the doctor. "Make sure the nurses don't do anything to clean him up."

"Sure."

"I'll alert the ME."

"Thanks." He studied her face as she pulled the sheet back over Donald's face. "Are you really the sheriff?"

Sharyn glanced at him. "Yes."

"Maybe you could help me? I've got this problem parking at my condo. The street is marked for parking on different sides for odd and even days during the winter. I have a problem getting into the parking deck. Maybe you could get me some kind of special privilege parking sticker so I don't keep getting tickets?"

She smiled. "I understand the problem, sir. Maybe the best answer would be to sell your car and consider public transport so you don't have to park at all."

He wasn't happy with the suggestion. "Thanks anyway. I hate the bus and the trolley is stupid."

"Sorry I couldn't be more help," she replied, still smiling. She nodded to Ernie and they started out of the room.

"Sorry I can't vote for you in the next election," the doctor mumbled.

"Idiot," Ernie muttered.

"What do you think?" she asked him.

"Huh? Oh." He rubbed the back of his neck. "Looks like suicide."

"Yeah. I guess that's it."

Ernie stared ahead. "I guess so. Are we heading to the motel?"

"Yes. We'll have to follow up on this anyway."

"I know."

They reached the outside of the hospital. The cold wind was welcome after the antiseptic smell of the emergency room and the sight of Donald Richmond on the table.

"I had something I wanted to ask you," Sharyn began as

they walked towards her Jeep. "Have you thought about running for sheriff in the next election?"

"Against you?"

"No," she hypothesized. "Say if I decided not to run for re-election." They were standing in the parking lot. The first faint snow flurries were falling around them from the gray sky.

Ernie faced her seriously. "Are you telling me that you aren't running?"

"Maybe," Sharyn answered.

"Is this a joke? Are you seriously thinking about not running for office again?"

"Yes." Sharyn took a deep breath and let it out. It turned to mist in the cold between them.

"I see." He looked out at the broad expanse of the lake that was visible from the hospital. "Any special reason?"

Sharyn looked down at her hands. "Maybe I just wasn't cut out for this, Ernie."

Ernie looked at her closely, wondering what was bothering her. "You're a better sheriff than your daddy, and that's no lie. He was good but you're better. What else would you do?"

She shrugged. "Go back and get my license to practice law."

"And you think I should be sheriff?"

"I think you wouldn't run before because of the Jefferson school secret hanging over your head. But it's out now and you didn't do anything wrong. You'd be a great sheriff."

"I appreciate your confidence," he said, looking away from her face. "But I wouldn't run for sheriff. If you leave, I'm right behind you."

"But you just got things straight with Annie!"

"Let me tell you something, ma'am. Some people are meant to take the lead. They're meant to be out in front. You're one of those people. I'm not and I don't want to be. I want to retire twenty years from now with you still sheriff. I know Joe and Ed feel the same way. And since David doesn't have a brain, he doesn't count."

"Ernie—"

"Sharyn, whatever's bothering you, don't let it. If it's Jack Winter, we'll find a way to get rid of him. If it's people like that doctor in there or Foster Odom, you're gonna have to work with people like that whether you're a lawyer or a sheriff. If it's your mother, she doesn't know what she's talking about!"

She shook her head and smiled at him. "You know you called me Sharyn."

He smiled his Ernie half-smile. "I know. This was personal."

"When is it professional?"

"Are we heading to the motel to check out the scene?" Yes."

"Then it's professional again, Sheriff. I'm ready when you are."

Sharyn laughed. "You're really something, you know."

He winked at her. "So are you, ma'am. I'll ride with you."

The Bridge Motel got its name from a failed attempt to build a bridge across the lake. It had been run down for as many years. Sharyn looked at it and considered what she'd told her mother about public eyesores. If any place qualified, it seemed to be this one. Half of the rooms were closed off with signs saying they were unsafe. The other half were little better than the remains of the old pylons and bridgework they stood beside.

"What was Donald Richmond doing here?" Sharyn wondered out loud as they walked towards the room where Joe and Ed were waiting for them.

"We may never know," Ernie returned, looking around at the shabby place.

"Glad you're here," Joe said, putting away his gun. "I was about to shoot the eyes out of that rat in the corner. It's as big as a chicken!"

"You didn't make it out to the mansion, did you?"

Ed shook his head. "Nope. We got the call after we picked up the search warrant and came right over."

"Any problem?" Sharyn wondered.

"Not with the warrant," Ed concluded. "But this place is pretty bad."

"We'll take it from here," she told them. "You two search those rooms. Donald Richmond is dead now. I'd like to know why."

"Guilt?" Joe suggested.

"If that's it," she agreed, "then we can close the case."

"What did Miz Eleanore have to say?" Ernie wondered.

"She told me about this." Sharyn showed them the letter from the insurance company.

"There's your motive," Ed reminded her. "Mr. Richmond knew he wasn't going to get that money so he hedged his bets. Then he felt guilty so he killed himself. Case closed."

"And that's why he wasn't worried about the money, why he was urging his wife to leave and forget the whole thing."

"So, he came back to Diamond Springs to challenge the will, thinking all the time that this insurance policy was his ace in the hole," Sharyn put it together out loud. "He saw things weren't going his way so he decided to go ahead and kill his wife to collect the money. In cold blood, he set this whole thing up months ago then executed her with poison and let a bear eat part of her. But then he felt guilty and decided to come down to this dive and shoot himself in the head. Is that about it?"

Ed looked at Joe. Joe shrugged. "We'll go on out to the mansion."

"Thanks. Make sure you bring back anything written down. I don't care what it's about."

"You got it," Ed replied.

"Did you find a weapon?" Ernie asked before they left.

"Right there on the floor where he dropped it when they moved him. It's a thirty-eight. Nothing special."

"Thanks!" he called out after them.

"I wonder where Nick is?" Sharyn asked, glancing at her watch.

"I called him," Ernie replied. "He should be here . . . better late than never!"

Nick strode quickly into the room. "Why did they move the body?"

"He wasn't a body just then, old son," Ernie assured him. "He died at the hospital. Where have you been?"

"Getting information about John Jackson as I was commanded by our gut-driven leader," he answered, putting on his gloves and taking out his tape recorder.

"So? You must have something?"

"Yeah. A headache. Anybody got any aspirin?"

Sharyn tapped her foot impatiently. "Anything else?"

"The county ME for Elkton told me in no uncertain terms that there was no reason to do an autopsy on John Jackson's body so they didn't. Nothing. He was released to the county right after they found him. There was no family. He was buried the next day."

"And he died in a skiing accident?"

"Massive trauma to his face and head. They think he might have been drinking because he was a great ski instructor and should have been able to dodge trees. It happened at night. They think he just didn't see the tree coming."

"Skiing at night," Ernie commented. "That makes as much sense as putting that old bridge across the lake."

"I assume this was the gun?" Nick asked. He picked up

the weapon carefully with his gloved hand. "I can give you the serial number."

Ernie took it down. "Be right back. We can at least see where he got it from."

"This kind of blows your theory, doesn't it?" Nick asked Sharyn when Ernie was gone.

"It still doesn't make sense to me. Why bother coming back if he didn't think he could win the suit for the money? Why not stay where he was? There was no record of them having problems out there."

Nick shrugged as he got down on his knees to get a blood sample from the place on the carpet where they'd found Donald Richmond. "I don't know. Maybe he thought he'd try to get the money. Darva was from Montana. Maybe he thought they'd ask more questions there."

"I picked up an insurance policy notice from Darva's aunt. It's made out to Donald for five million dollars. It was taken out the day he got word that he wasn't going to inherit."

Nick sat back on his heels. "Well, I don't see any sign of a struggle here. I haven't seen the body but the gun appeared to have been fired once. There was blood on the weapon so we know it was close range. Without knowing the circumstances, I'd say one to the head?"

"Yes."

Nick nodded. "I don't see any attempt to cover up blood splatter. It appears he didn't lay here long before he was found. He was still alive when they got here. Who called the police?"

"The motel owner called it in," Ernie said as he came back into the room. "The gun is registered to Darva Richmond. She bought it at a store in Elkton right after John Jackson was found dead."

Nick looked at Sharyn. "Autopsy?"

"Definitely."

"Two in one week," he quipped. "The county commission won't like that!"

"All they have to do is keep people from dying around here," she replied.

"Keep this closed off for now until I take a look at the body," Nick said, putting everything away in his bag. "I should have something preliminary for you before the end of the day."

"Thanks, Nick," Sharyn said. "I think we'll go and have a talk with the motel owner before we go."

"It would've been easier to determine everything if Richmond had been dead when they found him," Nick remarked sarcastically.

"You might not have felt that way if it was you," she answered.

"Maybe. I'll get back with you on that. What do you want to do about the Jackson guy?"

"Nothing right now. Let's solve our own problems first."

"What's the motel owner's name?" Sharyn asked as she and Ernie went to the office a few rooms down.

"Martin," Ernie said, consulting his notebook.

Sharyn knocked on the door, watching as the paint flakes flew down.

"Yeah?" A man answered. He was wearing a tattered T-shirt and dirty jeans.

"I'm Sheriff Sharyn Howard and this is Deputy Ernie Watkins. We're here to talk to you about the death in your motel."

"Yeah?"

"You called it in?" she wondered.

"Yeah."

"About what time was that?"

"About this morning when I heard the shot."

"You don't know what time?"

"I was sleeping, not looking at my watch."

"Did you see or hear anything, Mr. Martin?"

"I heard arguing then a loud sound, like a gun shot."

"What did you do then?"

"First, I yelled for them to shut up. When I heard the gunshot, I got up and was ready to hurt someone. I saw this woman run out of the room so I knew which room it was. I walked in and the man was laying on the floor, getting blood all over my rug."

"But you heard arguing first?"

"Yeah."

"Could you describe the woman?" Ernie asked.

"No, not really. Nothing special, I guess. I wasn't awake yet but I would've noticed a real looker."

"Do you think she was the one arguing with the man in that room?" Sharyn wondered. She knew the best she could hope for was speculation but it might still give some answers.

"I couldn't swear to it. People who live here aren't always quiet and nice like the people at The Regency, Sheriff. We get some fights and we've had a few suicides. I think it's the bridge."

Sharyn smiled. "What about how she left? Did you notice what kind of car she was driving? Did she leave on foot?"

He shrugged. "Couldn't say. I just didn't notice anything else after I saw the blood. I came back here and called the cops."

"Any reason you didn't call from that room?" Ernie wondered curiously.

"Dead guys bother me."

"He wasn't dead," Ernie said.

"He looked dead, Deputy. I came back here."

"Thanks for your help, Mr. Martin," Sharyn told him. "If you think of anything else, please give me a call." She handed him her card.

"That really your phone number?" he asked her.

"Yes."

"Okay." He shrugged. "Some people might pay some money for this."

"It's not my personal number," she corrected him. "Please leave the room the way it is until you hear from us. Thanks."

"So he didn't really see anything besides the dead guy he was afraid of," Ernie recapped as they walked away.

"He saw a woman."

"Who might or might not have come from the room."

"He thought he heard arguing before the gunshot."

"That might or might not have come from this room."

"Hey, Sheriff?" Mr. Martin called from the doorway of the motel office.

"Yes?" She stopped to face him.

"I think she had dark hair. The woman I saw. She was small and had dark hair."

"Thanks, Mr. Martin."

Ernie raised his eyebrows. "I know what you're thinking. But I can't imagine Julia Richmond down here."

"Let's see what Joe and Ed turn up at the mansion."

They separated at the hospital. Sharyn followed Ernie into the parking lot. The snow had stopped rolling down from the mountain but the temperature had dropped. The sky was no less threatening but it appeared to be waiting for the weather forecaster's prediction for that evening. The construction workers inside the lot were closing down for the day. Charlie was supervising them with a watchful eye.

Sharyn parked her Jeep and started in out of the bone-biting chill when a construction worker hurried up beside her. He lunged towards her, dangling a hammer in one hand and a backpack in the other. Ernie glanced towards Sharyn and saw him move. He shouted out a warning and ran towards her. Charlie heard the commotion and came running up through the lot.

Catching the movement from the corner of her eye, Sharyn stepped out of the worker's way. She pivoted and kicked the back of his left leg out from under him, following him down to the frozen ground with her knee in his back. He made a loud whooshing sound when his chest hit the ground. The hammer and the backpack flew out away from him. His hard hat followed, rolling across the lot away from him.

Ernie was already there. He kicked the backpack further away. Charlie wheezed up behind Sharyn, drawing his gun from its holster.

"Get off me!" Foster Odom yelled. "You're violating my civil rights!"

"You don't have any rights when it looks like you're pulling a gun on the sheriff," Ernie informed him abruptly.

"I was just trying to ask her a few questions! I sneaked in the lot and I wanted some answers."

"This could've been anyone," Ernie told Sharyn, his eyes worried. "If he'd had a gun, you might be dead right now."

The gathering crowd of construction workers drew more attention, bringing Trudy's head out of the door. "What's wrong?" she demanded.

"Nothing. We got it," Ernie replied.

"This is my fault," Charlie said with a shake of his head, putting away his gun. "You need a real security man back here. Not just a retired cop with a touch of rheumatism. I didn't see him sneak in. Ernie's right. It could've been a terrorist with a bomb or anything."

"Calm down," Sharyn recommended. "We don't really get many terrorists out here. Mr. Odom is just an ordinary citizen looking for some answers."

"That's right!"

". . . who's going to spend the night in jail and pay a

two-hundred-and-fifty-dollar fine for sneaking in here." She finished and pointed to the sign at the gate. "This area holds crime scene property and stolen cars. It's off-limits to anyone who's not a member of the sheriff's department."

"Give me a break!" the reporter complained as Sharyn let him up off the ground.

"If you want answers to questions, make an appointment."

"You'd never see me," he complained.

"You don't know that until you try," she answered. "Charlie, will you escort Mr. Odom off the property."

"What about jail and the fine?" he asked.

"I'll give you twenty-four hours to get your things together. Then you'll have to turn yourself in."

Odom glanced at Ernie and Sharyn. "You're kidding, right?"

"I wish she was," Ernie protested.

"I'm not. Bring a certified check for two hundred and fifty dollars and a toothbrush," she told the reporter. "Turn yourself in by tomorrow night."

Foster Odom considered the possibilities. "Great. All right. I'll be here."

Charlie took the man roughly by the arm and started walking him off the property.

"What was that all about?" Ernie wondered.

She shrugged. "Giving him a chance to see first-hand how the system works."

"Couldn't he have seen right now? You're not taking this seriously enough!"

"And you worry too much," she retorted. "Now let's go inside before we freeze out here!"

"Sheriff," Trudy hailed her before she could reach her office. "That's Herb Bennet." She pointed to the man in the rough plaid jacket. He was holding a cup of coffee and looking out the window. "He's here to report a missing person and since everyone was out, I had him wait."

"Thanks, Trudy," Sharyn replied.

After taking off their jackets, Sharyn and Ernie approached the man. He took off his dirty baseball cap and nodded his graying head. "I know you from your pictures, Sheriff," he told her with a tobacco-stained smile. "You're even prettier in person."

"Thank you, Mr. Bennet. This is Deputy Watkins. Would you like to come into the conference room?"

"Thanks."

"What does the problem seem to be, sir?" she asked him when they were seated in the room.

"Well, it's my daughter, Sylvia. I hate to bother you with this, Sheriff, but my wife and I have looked everywhere for her and we can't find her."

"How long has she been gone?" Sharyn wondered.

"About two weeks, I guess."

"And how old is she?"

"About your age, I reckon. She turned twenty-five this past February."

Ernie leaned forward. "Did she have any friends we could talk to, Mr. Bennet? Anybody she might have run off with?"

"No. She kept pretty much to herself. Me and her mother and her brother, T-Bone. We all keep to ourselves."

Sharyn took a deep breath. "Where do you live, Mr. Bennet?"

"Outside Claraville."

Ernie glanced at Sharyn. "Your daughter isn't under age, Mr. Bennet. She's been missing a good while but the best we can do is look for her. If we find her, it will be up to her if she wants to come home."

"Oh, she'll want to come home," Herb Bennet assured them. "She's a good girl."

"I'm not doubting that, Mr. Bennet."

"Do you have a picture of her?" Sharyn asked quietly.

The man drew a small, black-and-white picture from his pocket. It was worn and creased but the girl's features were clear enough to get an idea of what she looked like. Sharyn took it from him and put it down on the table. "What was she doing the last time you saw her, sir?"

"She was on her way to Diamond Springs to go to a museum. We dropped her off at the bus stop and we were supposed to pick her up that night. But she never came back."

"What museum?" Ernie queried.

"I'm not sure what the name of it is but they have quilts. She wanted to see those quilts because she and her mama are making one together. I tried to talk her out of it. Diamond Springs is a bad place. Bad things happen here. I didn't want my little girl to be lost here."

"We'll look for her, sir," Ernie promised. "If you'll leave us your phone number—"

"I don't have no phone," the other man said shortly. "My neighbor gave me this." He held out a slip of envelope. "This is his number and my address."

"Does Sylvia have anything unusual about her?" Sharyn asked before he left. "Birthmarks or scars?"

"She has a kind a strange mole and a little scar on her nose from where a tire swing hit her when she was a young 'un."

"Thank you, sir. I'll put someone on this and we'll let you know if we find anything."

"Thank you, Sheriff." He shook her hand heartily. "Thank you, Deputy."

Ernie walked him to the front door. Foster Odom was already there with his camera and his tape recorder.

"What am I supposed to do with him?" Trudy asked Sharyn.

"Send him downstairs to jail," Sharyn answered. "He's in overnight and make sure he has his check for two hundred and fifty dollars."

"Sheriff Howard," the reporter hailed her. "I'm ready. Take me away."

Joe and Ed walked in through the back, each carrying a basket full of papers and receipts. "They must have had a ton of credit cards," Joe remarked.

"Take them through to the conference room," Sharyn said. "Trudy, have someone from downstairs come up for Mr. Odom."

"What about you, Sheriff? Don't I get a chance to interview you?"

"I'm afraid not, Mr. Odom. Have a good night, sir."

"Sheriff! I thought . . . you seemed like . . ."

Sharyn turned away from him. "Trudy, will you put out a missing person's report on Sylvia Bennet?" She laid out the woman's picture. "Let me know right away if you hear anything."

"I will," Trudy promised, picking up the picture.

They sat down at the big table together and began to sift through the paperwork of two lives. There were receipts from clothes stores. Lots of clothes stores. Joe assured them that they had the clothes to prove it at the mansion.

They kept the important legal papers to one side. There were no other letters to Darva's aunt or anything that related to their time at the mansion. They had their marriage license and Darva's birth certificate. There were country club memberships and their car registrations. Darva's high school diploma was on the table alongside Donald's diploma from Diamond Springs High School.

"What were we expecting to find here, Sheriff?"

"I don't see whatever it is," Joe said.

Ernie whistled through his teeth. "Looks like Mrs. Rich-

mond had a considerable amount of insurance on Mr. Richmond, too."

"They had the money for it," Ed told him. "Look at the
bills they paid!"

"Look at their bank statement!" Joe added. "I won't see
that much money in my life! Why'd they want any more?"

"People always want more," Sharyn said. "How much
insurance, Ernie?"

"Two million," Ernie replied. "But it's made out to her.
Won't do anyone much good now."

"It might. Who's the next beneficiary?" Sharyn queried.

"It doesn't say."

"I've got their lawyer's name here in Diamond Springs,"
Sharyn said. "And the way this letter sounds, they had a
pretty good case. Ernie, would you give them a call and
let's see how good the case was? Then let's find out who
gets the money now."

"Sure." He took the paper from her.

"Thanks, Ernie."

He shrugged and went to his office. Joe and Ed were
called out to handle two separate wrecks on the Interstate.
It was almost five P.M. Sharyn stretched her back and flexed
her neck. The pile of papers that weren't important kept
growing.

It was getting increasingly difficult to know what she
was looking for. Darva and Donald Richmond were both
dead. Darva was killed by her jealous husband then he
killed himself. Why did that seem so wrong to her? And if
it was something else, why couldn't she see it?

"You're asking the wrong questions," she answered herself, looking through a few more papers.

"I talked to the lawyer, Sheriff," Ernie said to her. "He
said the case was really strong for Donald to get at least
half of the Richmond money. It would have been tied up

for years because most of it was in property and bonds and Julia has a team of lawyers. No word on the insurance yet."

"So, he wanted it faster." Sharyn sighed. "I guess I'm just going to have to accept that."

"He fooled me too," he consoled her. "We can't always judge using our instincts."

"I guess you're right," she agreed, half-heartedly.

"Sheriff?" A young woman from the computer department downstairs knocked on the door. "There's been this glitch in the system. It's small and I thought it was the system itself but—"

"Come on in," Sharyn invited, putting down the papers she was holding. "Cari, isn't it?"

"Yes, ma'am." The girl blushed prettily and glanced at Ernie. "Deputy Watkins."

"Cari."

"What's this about a glitch?"

"It's the fingerprints we put through the system for Donald Richmond, ma'am. There's something wrong with them."

Chapter Nine

"Something like what?" Sharyn asked.

"Well, ma'am, I ran his prints. It's standard procedure and even though we all know who Donald Richmond is, I thought I should do it anyway. He was arrested for murder and all. Was that wrong? I—I wasn't trying to second guess or anything—"

"Take a deep breath," Sharyn said to the nervous young woman. "What happened?"

"The fingerprints we took from him were on file. Not under his name. The system said that those weren't his fingerprints."

"Are you sure?"

Cari shook her head. "Yes, ma'am. I ran them through twice. I thought it was a glitch until I just ran the reporter's prints and they showed up just fine, along with his arrest for DWI three years ago. I ran Mr. Richmond's prints again and got the same thing."

"What did you get, Cari?" Sharyn asked

"This." The woman handed the printout to Sharyn.

Sharyn glanced at it and jumped to her feet. "Ernie! We were looking in the wrong place!"

"What do you mean?" She handed him the paper. "The fingerprints belong to John Jackson? He was arrested in Colorado for shoplifting and in Montana for passing bad checks."

Sharyn's cell phone rang. It was Nick.

"I finished the preliminary autopsy."

"What was his cause of death?"

"A bullet wedged in his left lobe that bled into his brain," Nick said sarcastically. "Were you expecting poison?"

"Will you check him for it?"

"For poison?"

"Will you check him for poison, please? I'll be right there." She closed the phone.

"Sheriff?"

"Go home, Ernie," she told him. "I'm going to see what happens with the autopsy."

"How can I go home not knowing?"

"I'll call if anything changes." She turned to Cari. "Thanks, Cari. You keep doing what's supposed to be done. It's procedure that makes it all work."

"Thank you, Sheriff," Cari said with a big smile. "I try to do a good job."

"This is a big help."

"Is now a good time to talk to you about the deputy trainee program?"

"Not really," Sharyn replied. "But if you'll fill out a form and leave it with Trudy, I promise, we'll talk."

"Thanks! That's great!"

Sharyn left Cari, still smiling, and went to get her jacket.

Ernie picked his up at the same time. "I'll call Annie," he said. "She'll understand."

"Ernie," Sharyn began then shook her head. "Never mind. I guess you'll have to know what's best for you."

"Thank you, Sheriff."

"But I'll fire you if you get all moony-eyed like you were before you left!"

"Moony-eyed? Like you'd know what that meant!"

"I know David," she reminded him. "I know what that means."

"Are you comparing me to *David*?"

"Ernie." David glanced at them as he walked into the office. His uniform was clean and pressed. His hair was combed and his face was clean-shaven except for the beginning of a mustache. He had a cut on his lip and a bruise under one eye but he looked alert and clear-eyed for once. "Sheriff."

"Looks like the snow might pass us by," Sharyn told him briefly. "JP is looking forward to working with you."

"Yeah," he intoned. "Me, too."

"You okay, son?" Ernie wondered, studying David's face.

"Just fine, now," David told him. "I've given up women. They do nothing but mess with a man's life."

"Excuse me, Sheriff?" Cari said, seeing they were still there. "You did say to put this on your desk?"

"Yes, that's fine," Sharyn replied.

"Deputy," Cari acknowledged David.

David took one look at her honey-colored hair and big brown eyes and decided that giving up *all* women was too drastic a step. He just needed to meet the *right* women. "I'm Deputy Matthews. David Matthews."

"Cari Long. I work downstairs in computers. But I want to enter the deputy trainee program."

"Well, I could be a big help to you there," he told her. "Just call me David."

Sharyn shook her head as the two walked towards the coffee break area. "I guess he's forgotten Julia."

Ernie laughed. "That boy would forget his own name if it wasn't on his shirt!"

They climbed in Sharyn's Jeep. The back lot was dark and empty but Ernie had been on guard when he walked out. "I'm gonna find some way to make this area safer," he told her. "After what happened—"

"Nothing happened."

"You're a stubborn cuss, Sheriff"

"Who brought it up again?"

Ernie sighed. "So what does it mean that the wrong prints were listed for Donald Richmond?"

"I'm not sure yet," she admitted. "But I have a feeling we're on the right track finally."

Nick was getting started with Donald's body as they arrived at the hospital morgue that had become the county medical examiner's office. Ernie shivered as he always did when they went there.

"I'm glad you came over," Nick said when he saw them. "Something strange has come up." He turned on a lighted screen and hung an X-ray on it. "You see this pin in Donald Richmond's leg? This afternoon when I was on the phone with the Elkton county coroner, he told me that he would fax me what information he did have on John Jackson. They didn't do anything when they had his body but I have some of his medical records. Look at this."

"What is it?" Ernie wondered, looking at the copy.

"A femur," Sharyn stated.

"Very good! Look at this." Nick pointed out for them. "This pin in Donald Richmond's knee looks exactly like the same pin and the same place where John Jackson was injured in a ski accident a few years before he died. I couldn't find any recent records for Richmond but no two injuries and pins would be exactly the same."

"And his fingerprints," Sharyn added. "They ran through the system and came back with this." She showed him the printout Cari had given her. She looked at the covered body on the table. "This man is John Jackson."

"How's that possible?" Nick wondered.

"Did you get a picture of him?"

"Black and white, kind of grainy." He took it out of his file and showed it to her.

"Similar facial features," Ernie considered. "If his hair was blond and he was dressed the same—"

"And no one had seen him in twenty years," Sharyn added.

"But Darva dated John Jackson before she married Donald Richmond. I think she would've known the difference," Ernie argued. "He could fool everyone here because his brother was dead and no one else had seen him in so long. But not a woman who'd known him intimately."

"Which would mean Darva was involved," Sharyn theorized.

"Or the old lady had her facts mixed up," Ernie guessed. "Maybe Darva told her that she'd known John Jackson before her marriage but she really didn't meet him until later."

"That wouldn't explain how she couldn't tell them apart," Nick remarked.

"Darva had to be involved, either willingly or unwillingly. She had to know that this man was really John Jackson."

"Maybe that's how she ended up dead," Ernie said.

Nick cleared his throat. "My question would be if this is John Jackson, who's in the grave with his name on it?"

Ernie looked at Sharyn. "The man with the money?"

"Darva and John hatched a scheme to get at the Richmond fortune?"

"But it was taking too long and Darva wasn't happy. So Jackson killed her."

The three of them looked at each other.

"There's only one way to know for sure," Nick said.

"Somebody has to dig up John Jackson's body and check to see if he's really Donald Richmond."

Sharyn drew in a deep breath. "He's buried in Montana."

Nick shrugged. "They'll have to exhume him and at least check his fingerprints. I've got a few other things they could check from Donald Richmond's childhood, injuries, et cetera. He was in the military for two years. When we get that information, we'll have his blood type and fingerprints."

"What about checking Jackson for poison?"

"I sent it to the lab. It'll be twenty-four hours before I know for sure. I can tell you that the wounds and powder marks on his head and hand are indicative of suicide. The bullet came in close but lodged in the brain. It did so much damage, I think it bounced back off the skull, there was no way he could've survived."

Sharyn nodded. "All right. I'll see what I can do about getting in touch with the authorities in Montana. Have you released Darva's body yet?"

"No, but I plan to tomorrow."

"Not yet," she told him. "Let's hold off on that."

"Okay. Anything else?" Nick wondered.

"Thanks, Nick. I think that's all I need from you. Let me know about the poison?"

"Sure."

"Well, that makes more sense why Darva was killed," Ernie remarked as they walked out of the hospital basement.

"I still can't see someone who could set up something this elaborate as being remorseful. It would mean he had killed Donald Richmond, taken his place, then come here to claim his life and his money. Darva went along with it as far as she could, then when she got cold feet, Jackson killed her, too. Then in a sudden fit of remorse, he killed himself."

Ernie yawned. "I can't figure it either. Darva had to know. Are you thinking that someone killed Jackson now?"

"We have the woman running out of the motel," Sharyn reminded him. "Maybe there was someone else involved in the scheme." She let him out at the parking lot behind the office. "I'll see you in the morning, Ernie." She waited while he got into a sheriff's car and left the lot. Then she drove slowly back to her house. Kristie and her mother were both in bed when she got there. She let herself into the house, changed clothes and showered, then made herself a bowl of soup. She switched on the gas logs in the fireplace and sat down before it.

There was too much information, she considered, drinking chamomile tea with her tomato soup. A lot of it didn't add up with what they'd discovered about Donald Richmond and John Jackson. Why had Darva told Tad Willis that Donald had killed her lover in Montana? Darva had to know about the switch. Maybe it was her way of trying to tell someone what had happened. She might have been afraid for her life.

"Are you still up?" Kristie asked her sister in an undertone. She walked into their father's study and sat beside Sharyn.

"Yeah. Still trying to figure this thing out."

"The murder?" Kristie wondered.

Sharyn nodded.

"Don't you think it might be unhealthy to sit around and think about murder all the time?"

"You, too?" Sharyn grimaced. "Did Mom give you money to say that?"

"Mom?" Kristie asked. "What does she have to do with it?"

Sharyn looked down at her bowl of soup. "She asked me to quit being sheriff and go back to pass the bar."

"Why?"

"Because she said she's scared all the time that something's going to happen to me."

"But you said no, right?"

"I said I'd think about it," Sharyn admitted.

"She was wrong to say that to you, Sharyn. Anyone can see that you love what you do! You're so good at it, too! Dad would be so proud of you!"

"But it didn't start out to be this way," Sharyn told her with a smile.

"Lots of things don't start out to be the way they end up," Kristie told her softly. "That doesn't mean they're wrong! You're a great sheriff and Diamond Springs needs you right now. Things are changing here. Nothing is the same anymore."

"I know."

"You can help everyone get through it, Sharyn. You're strong and smart and brave. Just like Dad and Gramps. It's probably too bad that you weren't a man."

"Why?" Sharyn asked with a laugh.

"Because Mom wouldn't have objected then. She just gets upset that you don't want to be a deb or get married and give her grandchildren!"

Sharyn looked at her sister in the firelight. "When did you grow up?"

"Like you. When Dad died." Kristie squared her shoulders and tossed her mane of blond hair. "He was my dad, too. I might look like Mom but I think like him. I just don't let on to her!" She got up and kissed Sharyn's cheek. "Don't stay up too late."

"Thanks, Kristie," Sharyn whispered. "Goodnight."

Sharyn resolved finally to clear her mind and get some sleep. She didn't actually think she could do it but when her head hit the pillow, she was asleep. It was light outside when she opened her eyes again.

Nick was on the phone before she left the house. "I got

the results back. Richmond, or Jackson, if you prefer, had consumed a small amount of strychnine. Without the bullet, he probably would've been sick but not died."

"But it's not unusual for a suicide to use two methods," Sharyn replied as she tied her shoes.

"You got it. It was there but it doesn't prove anything."

"How was it consumed?"

"Wine again. Not the same kind."

"But I didn't see any sign of a glass or a bottle at the motel, did you?"

Nick considered the question. "No. Although he could have consumed it somewhere else and driven there to shoot himself. It could have caused him to lose consciousness but it's hard to say for sure."

Sharyn clipped on her badge. "I'll be at the office in a few minutes. Let's see what else we can dig up."

"You mean in Montana?"

"That's what I mean."

Sharyn spent the entire day being put on hold and shuffled from one official to another. She was able to get a court order from Judge White to have the body exhumed but the police chief in Elkton was not cooperative. Nick talked to the medical examiner but that was a dead end, too. The man didn't want to be held responsible if there was an error.

In the end, it came down to Sharyn making a call to the governor's office. At about two P.M., she heard back from the chief telling her that they would honor the order to exhume the body but anything else was up to her. The governor told her that he'd done what he could, she would have to do the rest.

"In other words, Nick, you're going to have to go to Elkton and do the autopsy. Or at least get the fingerprints and blood type. I've booked you on a flight for five this afternoon. That should give you time to pack and—"

"No."

"What?"

"I'm not going to Montana to do an autopsy! Would you like me to say it in Greek?"

"Why?" she wondered. "I cleared it with the county commission. They're willing to pay for the ticket and pay you for your time. I think it's because it's the Richmonds 'again."

"I don't care, Sharyn! I have a class later today and one tomorrow morning. There's no reason why I should go out there to get a few fingerprints and a blood sample! They can do it and fax it to us."

"They don't want to put out the money and they don't think any of it is true," she argued. "You have to go! We can't prove that body out there is Donald Richmond if you don't go!" She wished she had gone to his office and seen his face. Why was he being so stubborn?

"It's primarily fingerprints, Sharyn!" he complained. "Anyone could do it! I'm not going all the way out there for *that!*"

"Nick—"

"*No,* Sharyn! What does it matter anyway? They're both dead."

"The commission agreed with me that we have to know for sure that Donald Richmond is buried out there. Julia Richmond is leaning on a few of them to make sure that her brother-in-law is dead and won't be coming back to claim any money again. We need to know to close the file on this murder."

"No, Sharyn. I'm sorry. I won't go."

Sharyn looked at the phone after he'd hung up on her and the line had gone dead. She would never understand him. The one thing she did understand, however, was that someone had to go.

At ten after five that evening, Sharyn was on Flight 203

to Helena, Montana. After that, she was renting a car that would take her to Elkton. It sounded like a town that was even smaller than Diamond Springs, since their medical examiner was only there once a month. It was a hundred miles from the capital to Elkton. She was flying back at one in the morning.

It was a tight schedule. Sharyn stowed away her only bag that contained a change of clothes, a fingerprint kit and a camera. She sat down in the seat with her laptop, prepared to go over everything she had on the two cases on the two-hour flight to Helena. She didn't look up when someone sat beside her.

"I can't believe you didn't assign this to someone else," Nick said flatly.

Sharyn still didn't look up, although her heart bumped a little in her chest. She refused to think about her reaction. "There wasn't anyone else," she retorted. "After I couldn't find you this afternoon, I put Ernie in charge and packed my bag. Why are you here?"

"Ernie told me you were going."

"So he shamed you into coming to say goodbye?"

"I'm going, too," Nick stated. "Although you could've picked a decent plane."

"They didn't let me pick the plane, Nick. And there's not a lot of flights to Montana right now. I had to take what I could get. And I don't need you to go."

"I don't think they're going to refund my ticket money," he said. "I'm going."

"So Ernie shamed you into going?"

"Ernie didn't *shame* me into anything!" he responded angrily. "I came because you need me."

She finally looked up at him. "I can handle this without you."

"No," he said, his black eyes staring straight into hers. "You can't."

Sharyn didn't look away. "Would you have come if I'd sent Joe?"

"No," he answered in a fierce voice that was close to a whisper. "I wouldn't."

"Why?"

He looked away from her. The door to the plane was being closed and Nick shifted down in his seat. He groaned. "I wouldn't risk my life for Joe."

Sharyn watched him squirm in his seat and tighten his seatbelt several times. "What's wrong with you?"

"We're about to throw ourselves in the air in a heavy metal cylinder and you want to know what's wrong with me?"

It suddenly dawned on her. "You're afraid to fly?"

"Genius!"

"That's why I'm the sheriff." She settled back comfortably in her own seat. "I didn't know you were afraid of planes."

"I'm not afraid of planes themselves," he announced. "It's the flying part that bothers me."

"We aren't going to crash," she reassured him. The plane had begun moving down the runway and the pilot welcomed them aboard. "It's only a short flight."

"Like that has anything to do with it! Look around you! Does this look safe to you?"

"That's why you wouldn't come, no matter what?"

"Almost," he agreed. "I should have stayed on the ground. Why am I here?"

The plane was building up speed, moving down the runway. Sharyn saw the change in the movement outside the window as she felt the pressure when the plane began to lift skyward. She put her hand over Nick's that was clamped on the arm of the seat between them. "Tell me something," she urged.

"Like what?" he asked with his eyes closed.

She shrugged, not sure what to ask him. "Tell me why you got into forensics."

"*What?*"

"Okay. Tell me how many guns you have?"

"I collect guns."

"I noticed. How many have you collected?"

"Two hundred."

"Really? But they aren't all in your car, are they?"

"No. I keep most of them at my apartment."

"What's your favorite?'

"I don't know," he responded. "I suppose the Berretta."

"Why?"

"The weight and the way it handles. It's a smooth piece."

"When did you start collecting?"

"When I was in college." He opened one eye. "Are we up yet?"

"Yes."

He looked at her hand that covered his. "I really hate this!"

"I can see that."

"I appreciate you trying to help me with it."

Sharyn looked at him curiously. "How am I doing?"

He smiled. "I was . . . distracted."

"Good. Now about those guns—"

"Ernie told me about what happened in the parking lot yesterday."

"Nothing happened," she assured him. "It was only a reporter trying to get a story."

"I think you should replace Charlie with a competent security guard."

"Ernie shouldn't spread that stuff around."

"He was just trying to get me to back him on a new security plan for the lot."

She frowned. "So he's told everyone?"

Nick nodded. He paled and reached for the chair arms

when the plane dipped a little as it hit an air pocket. "Why don't we just have fast trains?"

"Have you ever been in a plane crash?" she asked him.

"No."

"Known someone who was?"

"Not exactly. Unless you count the first forensics job I ever did. It was a military transport plane. All two hundred people on board were killed when it ran into a mountain."

"That had to be bad," she admitted.

"It was gruesome."

"So, then you started collecting guns?"

He opened one eye again and glared at her through it. "You think this is funny, don't you?"

"No," she answered but she smiled as she said it.

"I knew it. That's okay."

"Thanks." She smiled a little more broadly.

"You can help with the autopsy."

"I don't know enough about forensics."

"I'm used to working with students. I'll teach you."

They landed at around seven P.M. The car was waiting for them. Sharyn drove to Elkton. Nick slept the whole way there. It was a long, dark drive down a deserted stretch of highway but she made good time because of it. In a little over an hour, they were in the town that boasted a population of two thousand, four hundred. The signs for the ski resort were bigger than the buildings, dominating everything else on the skyline.

Sharyn pulled over at the police station and turned off the car. Nick didn't wake up. She studied his features in the light from the illuminated ski resort sign that stood outside the station. His dark face was relaxed, his coat open in the warmth from the car's heater. A lock of black hair had fallen into his face. He twitched his nose and pushed at it with his fingers. Without thinking, Sharyn slid her hand across it, pushing it off of his forehead.

He smiled, then opened his eyes. "Are we there yet?"

"Just got here."

He nodded. "Good. I'm hungry. I need to eat before I can look at a dead body." She shuddered. "How can you lump the two together?"

"That's why I'm the medical examiner," he quipped. "Come on. We'll find your stubborn police chief, then we'll wander over to the local diner."

"We're only here until one," she reminded him.

"No problem, assistant. But thanks for reminding me."

They walked into the police station together. The silence was eerie in the snow-whitened landscape. Mountains that dwarfed the Uwharries rose like giants around them. The cold was piercing. Sharyn could feel that her jacket that was fine at home wouldn't stand up to a day here.

"I'd like to speak to the chief, please," she told the man on duty.

"He's over at Lou's getting the corpse settled in."

"Corpse?"

"Yeah, couple of people from back east want to see a dead guy. Lucky for them he was in a crypt because of them moving the cemetery or they would have had to wait 'til the summer!"

"Where's Lou's?" Nick asked.

"Across the street. Best cup of coffee in Elkton."

"It's a *restaurant?*" Sharyn determined.

"Yeah. It's the only place with a cooler big enough to keep a whole body." He looked up at them. "What did you want to see the chief about?"

"The dead guy," Nick told him. "And a cup of coffee. Thanks!"

They hurried across the icy street together. Unlike snow and ice in Diamond Springs that meant the town closed down, Elkton was full of tourists and skiers. The road was jammed with cars. People were walking down the old wooden sidewalk and dogs were barking as they ran with their owners. With the colored scarfs and flashy ski gear, it was like walking through a modern painting of a ski town.

Sharyn mentioned as much to Nick, who glanced around himself and shrugged. "I guess. I hope they have some good pasta."

"Is that all you can think of?"

"No. I'm hoping that the corpse isn't frozen solid."

"Never mind."

Police Chief Arthur Peabody looked at Sharyn's credentials with a sour face. "Well, he's *here*. What you do with him from *here*, is up to you."

Sharyn gave him the letter from Julia as Donald's next of kin that allowed her to exhume the body. "I think you'll find everything is in order."

"Unless this isn't Donald Richmond." He glanced at the document, then shoved it into his pocket. "Then you'll probably have John Jackson's family suing you."

"Does he have family up here?" Sharyn wondered.

"Not that we've been able to find," the chief told her bluntly. "Otherwise, you wouldn't have to be here. Who's he?"

"Dr. Nicholas Thomopolis," Nick said, offering his gloved hand to the man. "If you could show me where he is, I'll take it from there."

"Sure thing, Doc." The chief warmed to Nick immediately. "He's back here in the meat storage. There's a table you can use back here. Flo uses it to cut meat, so it should be good for you."

"Thanks."

"You know I went to school with a guy named George Thomopolis at Georgetown. You know him?"

"Sounds like my uncle," Nick said. "Big man. Skinny legs?"

"That's him! You never know who you're gonna meet, do you?"

The chief sat with them while Nick consumed a huge meal. He talked constantly to Nick about his uncle and forensics. He completely ignored Sharyn. She didn't care. She got down a grilled-cheese sandwich and some weak hot tea. She didn't much care about the man or his rudeness. She just wanted to get through the autopsy and go home.

"Are you ready?" Nick asked her finally.

She nodded. "Any time."

The chief left them, telling Nick it was a pleasure to meet him and barely glancing towards Sharyn. Nick gave Sharyn gloves, a mask, and a plastic apron. When they had both added the protective gear, she helped him pull the body from the cooler. It was on a metal tray that slid out easily. They maneuvered it onto the table and Nick turned on the overhead light.

"Good preservation," Nick said. "We should be able to get fingerprints without any problem."

"Lucky for us since that's about all we have to go on."

"I'm going to take some tissue samples and take them back with us to have checked for toxicology and typing. I'll bet we find strychnine." He pulled back the plastic sheet that still covered the face. "Whew! No wonder they couldn't identify him!"

"He was wearing some type of jewelry that was identified along with the ID in his pocket," Sharyn read from the statement.

"They should have checked him," Nick remarked.

"We had the same thing with Darva's body," she recalled. "Not really able to ID her by her face but she was wearing her ring and carrying her purse."

Nick looked at her. "That morning you were wondering why she was taking her purse to the bathroom with her."

"Maybe it was for ID. The same as this man."

"And after that first bear attack, I don't know if we would have done anything any different with Darva if hadn't noticed the honey congealed on her."

"Skiers smack into trees all the time, I suppose."

Nick nodded, putting his tissue sample into a small jar. "And though people aren't eaten by bears every day on Diamond Mountain, you wouldn't necessarily ask any questions."

"I still don't get it."

"Well, get this." He handed her the fingerprints he'd carefully made from the dead man's hand. "It's a match. This is Donald Richmond."

"Okay. We'll have to let Julia know. She wants him buried back home. She says Beau would have wanted it that way. I guess we'll give Mr. Jackson to the county for burial since he has no relatives."

"So, what now?" Nick wondered. "John Jackson must have killed Donald Richmond and taken his place to get the money, leaning heavily on that fact that they favored each other and that no one back home had seen Donald for years."

"And we know that Darva was involved with both of them."

"So Darva had to help out," Nick continued to speculate. "She must have wanted out and Jackson killed her."

"Yet, no one ever heard them arguing about *her* wanting to leave. It was always Jackson through the whole thing that said they could get along without Beau Richmond's money. Darva was the pusher."

"But she was the first one dead."

Sharyn considered the problem. There was no immediate answer. She shivered in the cold room. "Let's go home. Whatever the answer is, it's not here. I'm going to set up to have Donald's body flown back to Diamond Springs."

"Still not happy with the outcome?"

She shook her head. "Not until it makes sense."

Chapter Ten

The airport in Helena had been all but deserted when they got there to catch their flight at midnight. Julia Richmond had been thrilled to know that Donald was actually dead and more than happy to pay to have his body brought home. The officials in Elkton were glad to get rid of it, too. It would be on the next flight out.

Sharyn slept all the way back on the plane. She hadn't meant to fall asleep. It was like she was sitting there awake one moment, then she was asleep the next. She dreamed about roses and sneezing while she was running through a long, dark tunnel looking for Kristie.

Nick shook her a little when she started thrashing in her seat. She opened her eyes, put her hand on his face and smiled, then she went back to sleep. He caught himself, sitting there, watching her sleep. Then he cleared his throat and forced himself to look away from her freckles and pink cheeks. He opened the laptop and went through the information about the Richmond murder, until the pilot announced that they were landing.

The announcement woke Sharyn. She saw Nick putting away the laptop and rubbed her eyes. "What time is it?"

"Almost three A.M." he replied. "We're about to land."

"Sorry. I didn't mean to fall asleep."

"You didn't turn into a hideous beast or anything."

"You seem to have handled it all right."

"You mean the flight?" he wondered.

"You're not gripping the seat."

"And I'm probably not as pale as you were in that kitchen with Donald Richmond's body either. When did you get squeamish?"

"It was an unusual situation. It was a *kitchen*!"

He lifted one brow in question.

"It seems to be something that comes and goes," she explained finally. "I think it all depends on the case."

"Well, well!"

"What?"

"You finally admitted it!"

"Admitted what?"

"That you can't *always* do it all."

"I never said—"

"You didn't have to say it! You run into burning buildings. You confront killers without backup. You get yourself thrown in jail—"

"Holding," she corrected.

"You take unnecessary chances with your life. You don't have to be Superwoman!"

"I don't try to be Superwoman!"

"Your father never set foot in an autopsy room the whole ten years I worked with him. He couldn't stand the process. He didn't feel weak admitting it."

Sharyn hadn't known that about her father. "I don't mind admitting when I can't do something!"

"No wonder your mother wants you to give up being sheriff."

"She talked to you?"

He smiled wickedly. "She thinks of me as family. Especially now that we're dating."

"We aren't dating!"

"Try to tell her that!"

Sharyn shook her head. "So she told you about asking me not to run in the next election?"

"Yes."

"What did you say?" she asked quietly.

"I told her you were a good sheriff and that I'd keep an eye on you until you weren't so careless."

"You did *what*?"

"Why? Were you thinking about quitting?"

"Not really," she admitted. "A lot of things she said made sense. I didn't start out to be sheriff. It just happened."

"And?"

"And I'm not sorry. I like being sheriff. I'm just not sure—"

"Good." He nodded his head as he got up to leave the plane. "You've got my vote."

"Thanks. But I can't believe you told her you'd keep an eye on me."

Nick grinned. "She knows I have two hundred guns."

"Oh."

"Exactly."

Sharyn went home. She looked at her bed but it was almost five A.M. There didn't seem to be much point in going to sleep for an hour. The information they'd brought back from Montana didn't give her any peace. She still felt that something was wrong. It was all tied together somehow.

Trudy wasn't in yet when she reached the office. She looked through her files and read through computer information. There was a note that Eleanore Lacey had called and wanted to see Sharyn before she left town. Apparently the old woman had changed her mind about waiting for her niece's funeral. She searched her desk drawer for antihistamines she could take before she went to the hotel again.

The case was going to be closed. She couldn't justify spending any more time or money on it. Darva would be buried and John Jackson would be buried. Donald would be entombed in the Richmond family cemetery. And that would be the end to it.

Her report would have to read: *John Jackson killed Donald Richmond, probably with the help of Darva Richmond, who was having an affair with him. John, either in a fit of jealous rage or because Darva didn't want to be part of it anymore, killed her and tried to disguise her death as a bear attack. After realizing what he'd done, John Jackson consumed strychnine, then shot himself in the head.* End of report.

Maybe it was just that Jackson had gotten away with two murders, one right under her nose, that bothered her. She continued randomly going through the papers on the conference table. Maybe that was all that was bothering her.

She looked at the newspaper article that featured Darva at the fundraiser where they'd briefly met. Foster Odom had written the article that crowned her as one of the new young queens of Diamond Springs society. When she saw the picture of Darva, holding the full sheaf of roses, her bright eyes shining in the camera's lens, something inside of Sharyn snapped to attention. Nick's words during the autopsy suddenly hit her.

By the time Ed came in an hour later, Sharyn was going through all of the receipts they'd brought back from the mansion. "Sheriff?"

"Hi, Ed."

"What's up?"

"I know I saw some receipts in here for . . . yes! Here's

one." She pulled a piece of paper from the stack. "And another and another."

"What are you looking for?"

"Receipts, Ed."

"Joe moved back home with Sarah last night. I have a date with that new waitress down at the cafe."

"Great."

"I'm on patrol this morning."

"Okay."

He shrugged and left her alone with the receipts. Ernie found her still there but now she was on the phone. "Call Nick," she said, holding her hand over the receiver while she was on hold. "Tell him I need him to take another look at Darva Richmond."

"What's he looking for?"

"I'll explain in a minute."

Ernie got on the phone and finally managed to reach Nick at the college during a break between classes.

"I can't get there until after lunch," Nick told him. "What's up?"

"I'm not sure," Ernie answered.

"Is that Nick?" Sharyn asked quickly as she walked into Ernie's office.

"He says he can't be there until after lunch."

Sharyn took the phone. "Nick? I need you there in about an hour."

"Sharyn, you know I have classes!"

"Get one of your clever students to teach for you for a couple classes. I need you at the morgue!"

"All right. Fine. I'll be there." He hung up.

"Joe, I need you to go out to the Bennet farm outside Claraville. Bring Mr. Bennet back with you. Blue light, Joe! This is an emergency!"

"Sure thing! What's up?"

"I need him to ID a body."

"What's wrong?" Ernie asked when Joe left.

"I think there's been a mistake. And I'd like you to come with me to see Eleanore Lacey again. I took some antihistamines but those roses are driving my allergies crazy!"

"Sure thing," Ernie said. "But what are we doing?"

"Questioning a murder suspect."

"The old lady? Sheriff—"

"Come on, Ernie!"

But when they reached The Regency Hotel, Eleanore Lacey didn't answer her phone.

"I need to get in there," Sharyn told the manager.

"I'm afraid it's hotel policy—"

"I need to get in there *now*! This is official business, Mr. Bartlett, not a request! Don't make me break down the door!"

The manager glanced at Ernie, then shrugged his shoulders. "All right, all right, Sheriff! Just let me find the key!"

Sharyn drew her weapon at the door of Room 307.

Mr. Bartlett took a step back. "Sheriff!"

"I hope not to use it, sir. Please open the door!"

Ernie drew his gun, too, although he felt silly doing it. He was worried about scaring Miss Eleanore to death with their guns and breaking into her hotel room.

Mr. Bartlett opened the door with his master key, then started to go into the room.

Sharyn held him back. "Don't go in there, yet."

"Sheriff, this is ridiculous! Miss Eleanore wouldn't hurt a fly!"

"Just stay out here, Mr. Bartlett, or I'll arrest you!"

The manager drew a deep breath, hoped he didn't get sued, and stepped aside for the sheriff to enter the room first.

Sharyn went in cautiously. Ernie followed her. She was pretty sure what she would find but she didn't want to take any chances. When she saw the wig, make-up, and Miss

Eleanore's cane on the table, she put away her gun. Beside the wig was a vase full of roses.

"Looks like Miss Eleanore left in a hurry," she said, pulling on her gloves. "Get on the phone, Ernie. See if she booked a flight out under her name or someone else's."

"I don't understand," the manager said, reaching for the gray hairpiece.

"Please don't touch that, sir. I'll need this room cordoned off for an investigation. If you could check your records for me, please, and find out how Miss Eleanore paid for this room?"

"Of course." The manager puzzled for a moment, troubled by the whole occurrence. "Is she dead?"

"That particular personality might be," Sharyn told him. "I really need those records before I leave here, sir."

"Yes, of course."

Sharyn picked up the gray wig. She glanced at the roses on the table but her antihistamines were holding so far. She wasn't sneezing. There was a note addressed to her in a rose-covered envelope. She opened it and a shower of rose petals fell to the floor at her feet.

It was fun while it lasted!

"There's no Eleanore Lacey booked on any flight out of Charlotte airport," Ernie told her with the phone still attached to his ear. "You want me to check something else?"

"What was Darva's maiden name?" Sharyn asked as she carefully put everything on the table into a bag.

"Uh—I don't recall!"

Sharyn got on her cell phone. "Trudy? Do me a favor and look up Darva Richmond's maiden name."

"Right away," Trudy replied, getting on the computer.

"Miss Eleanore paid in cash, in advance," Mr. Bartlett

returned to tell her. "Will someone please tell me what's going on?"

"Did you ever see any ID?" Sharyn asked.

"Well, no, I—"

"Darva's maiden name was Pryer," Trudy told her. "Darva Pryer."

"Thanks, Trudy." Sharyn closed her cell phone. "Check for Pryer, Ernie. Darva Pryer."

Ernie spoke into the phone.

"What about Miss Eleanore?" Mr. Bartlett asked.

"There is no Miss Eleanore," Sharyn told him. "Ernie?"

"D. Pryer," Ernie answered. "She's booked on the next non-stop flight to Jamaica. Ten-thirty this morning."

"Let's move!" Sharyn returned.

"Sheriff!" Mr. Bartlett called.

"Don't touch anything. Keep this door locked. Get everyone else out now!" She walked past the gawking maid and the curious luggage attendant.

When they reached the sheriff's car, Ernie got in the driver's seat.

Sharyn flicked on the lights and siren. "Let's go!"

"So Darva Richmond is alive!"

"She scammed us, Ernie. She scammed everyone."

"But how?"

"She killed Sylvia Bennet with strychnine, then put her body where she could get to it easily that night. Probably the dumpster where they found that piece of her robe. It stayed cold outside, so it made time of death look delayed. Then, she told John Jackson, who was masquerading as her husband, that she was going outside to the bathroom, probably because she did something to the toilet inside the trailer. She took Sylvia's body out, put her clothes on her and poured the honey and bear attractant on her. The mother bear wasn't far behind."

"Why?"

"We already know she and Jackson were lovers. They plotted to kill Donald to be able to get at his money. Donald and John were similar in height, weight, and build. No one knew Donald in Montana, so it was easy to replace him. Then when Beau died, they took a calculated risk and came back here to challenge the will."

"That would be mighty brazen of them," Ernie replied.

"She's been mighty brazen, Ernie!" Sharyn handed him the fax she'd received that morning. "Miss Eleanore told us what a good actress Darva was. I suppose she thought she could fake it since Donald's brother was dead and no one else here had seen him for a long time. Donald had been a loner and an outsider for all of his life. It made it easier for Darva."

Ernie glanced at the fax from the insurance company. "Eleanore Lacey is the recipient of both insurance policies on the Richmonds?"

"You got it."

"She stood to inherit about seven million."

"Yes. She wasn't willing to take the chance that something could happen at the last minute that would prevent her from getting her hands on Donald's money. After all, the real Donald was dead. So she had a back-up plan."

"And she didn't want to share."

"Exactly. Jackson had been whining about leaving the mansion. So she made it look like she'd been murdered. Everything pointed to Donald. Or rather, Jackson. She might have thought that he'd crack and tell us that he was really John Jackson but he stood firm as Donald. That wasn't working for her either. She came here as Eleanore Lacey to lead us along the right path so that John would be found out and convicted of both murders. She arranged to meet John at the motel on the lake, probably pretending to be Julia since the owner saw a dark-haired woman leave the room. She slipped him enough strychnine to make it easy to overpower him, held his hand on the gun, and pulled the trigger. She wanted it to look like a suicide, so this time she cleaned up after herself."

Ernie shook his head as he raced down the crowded highway. "And she knew about your allergy to roses from that night you met at the banquet!"

"And she used it against me," Sharyn agreed. "We were so sure Darva was dead, just like the police in Elkton thought John Jackson was dead. Nick remarked about how they'd used Jackson's ID to set the whole thing up. I started thinking about Darva's purse lying on the ground at the scene. Everyone thought it was just something a woman would do. When Darva and I talked at dinner, she told me she never carried a purse. I remembered again when I saw the picture of her from that night at the dinner. No purse. She was betting on us being uninterested, like the police in Montana. Especially since I couldn't even be in the room with her without sneezing."

Sharyn showed him the receipt that she'd seen in Darva's papers. "This is what tipped me off after I saw the picture of Darva from that night at the banquet. It was the roses. I knew Eleanore Lacey had to be wearing an essential oil for me to react so strongly. Darva ordered a ton of it from a place on the Internet. I saw the same bottles on Miss Eleanore's table at the hotel. That night at the banquet, it was the roses right up in my face. Darva used the essential rose oil to keep me from looking too closely, hoping it would also make me want to close the case quickly."

Sharyn's phone rang. It was Nick. "Brace yourself," he told her. "Mr. Bennet is here with his wife. They've identified the body as their daughter Sylvia. I didn't say anything, just let them look at her. She had a star-shaped mole on her back. They took one look and knew it was her. Or am I telling you something you already knew?"

"Yes and no," Sharyn sad sadly. "If you're done with

their daughter, Nick, release her to them. I think we know everything we need to from her and there's no point in making them suffer anymore. I'm sorry you had to go through that alone."

"Joe was here, too," he said. "Where are you?"

"Ernie and I are going to the airport. Darva is on her way out of town to Jamaica at ten-thirty."

He whistled. "That doesn't give you much time, does it?"

"No. I'm going to call and alert airport security now, so I'll talk to you later."

"Sure. Sharyn? Be careful."

"I will. Thanks, Nick."

"Joe wants to know if you need him there," Nick repeated the deputy's words.

"There isn't enough time. Tell him to hold down the fort until we get back."

"You got it."

Sharyn hung up and called airport security, telling them what flight Darva would be on and giving them her general description. She looked at the phone thoughtfully when she'd finished. "If she looks like Darva again."

"You think she might try another disguise?"

"I don't know. She's clever, Ernie. She knows she has a head start but she might not take any chances. After all, she wasn't prepared for this. She left in a hurry. Everything was going her way. I wonder what tipped her off?"

"She found out you went to Montana. Maybe she was afraid you'd come back with too much information."

"I don't know," Sharyn replied. "But we can't lose her now."

Ernie pulled the sheriff's car up to the front of the main concourse building. A throng of security agents met them and introduced themselves. They accompanied Sharyn and Ernie inside. They'd held the plane to Jamaica so that it couldn't leave the airport. The passengers were trapped inside, waiting for permission to leave.

Sharyn and Ernie walked carefully down the aisles of the plane but there was no sign of Darva or Eleanore Lacey. Passenger D. Pryer was not on board.

"It was another ruse," Sharyn decided. "We need a computer!"

They peered at the computer screen while the security guards waited around them. The airport was busy but the area around the flight to Jamaica was kept off limits. Other passengers stared as they walked quickly by the large group.

"Bingo!" Ernie said loudly. "How about Eleanore Pryer?"

"It's worth a try," Sharyn said. "What flight?"

"Flight 101 to Brazil. It was supposed to leave at ten."

"We could still call it back," the head security guard told them. "Let's see if it's left yet."

The plane to Brazil had already gone. They watched it as it taxied down the runway but a security guard was already on the phone, alerting the pilot and crew that the plane would have to return. The pilot radioed back that they had discovered passenger Eleanore Pryer. She was on the plane.

It took an hour for the plane to stop, turn around, and taxi back to its original space. The crew stayed on board and the passengers were detained in their seats while Sharyn and Ernie were brought on the plane.

Passenger Eleanore Pryer was scared and nervous with all the attention from the gun-carrying security forces. It was easy to tell that she was the wrong woman. Even Darva couldn't successfully pretend to be an eighteen-year-old girl with a buzz clip and a nose ring!

"Is this her?" one of the guards asked.

"No," Ernie told him.

"Is your name Eleanore Pryer?" Sharyn asked the frightened young girl.

"No. The woman with this seat asked me to trade. This is first class." She smiled weakly. "I was in coach."

"Where?" Sharyn asked her while the security guards started to leave the plane.

"Towards the tail. F 12."

"If she's gone, we'll have to alert the FBI," one of the marshals told Ernie. He looked around. "Where's Sheriff Howard?"

Sharyn wished she could disguise herself. The best she could do was walk back through the plane towards the tail and hope that Darva panicked when she saw her. It seemed unlikely. Darva hadn't been able to leave. She had to be on board. She could have changed seats ten times already and might have been sitting a row back from her original seat.

She sniffed the re-circulated air. The essential rose oil was powerful and would have been difficult to remove from her skin and clothes. Darva left in a hurry with only enough time to mock her pursuers. With any luck—

Sharyn felt her nose twitch as she walked past the galley.

"Can I help you, ma'am?" a flight attendant asked. "You should be in your seat. We'll be taking off momentarily."

The flight attendant wasn't wearing rose oil but the scent lingered, teasing Sharyn's allergies. "What's through there?"

"That's where we prepare the meals but—"

Sharyn walked back through the opening, looking carefully through the boxes of food and drinks that were used on the flight.

"You can't just go back there!"

"I'm here with security," Sharyn told her briefly before she heard someone groan.

She knelt down beside a woman who was lying on the

floor. Sharyn began to sneeze as she tried to examine her. The woman was wearing only her pink slip but in a heap beside her were Darva's clothes, saturated in rose oil.

"That's Allison!" the other flight attendant told her. "What happened?"

"Stay with her," Sharyn told her between sneezes.

Darva was dressed in the plain blue/gray of a flight attendant. She still couldn't leave the plane.

"Sheriff?" Ernie said, reaching her. "The security team is ready to leave."

"She's here, dressed like a flight attendant," she told him, sniffling. "We have to—"

Sharyn caught sight of her hurrying towards the door and ran after her. Darva raised a gun and the people around them screamed and tried to get on the floor. Sharyn threw herself down the aisle at her, knocking Darva down.

The security guards and the marshals crowded into the compartment. People were still screaming and crying around them but Sharyn didn't let go of Darva.

"It's not real," Darva said with a laugh when they'd picked her up from the floor. She waved her hands. "It was only plastic. Don't you have any faith in the security system?"

Ernie nodded, holding the gun in his hands. "It's not real."

"You're still under arrest, Darva," Sharyn told her.

"You can't prove any of it," she told them. "I want a lawyer!"

"Let me tell you your rights first, Miz Richmond," Ernie said, putting cuffs on her wrists. "You were just one step too clever for your own good."

"Ten steps more clever than *you,* Deputy!" she proclaimed, straightening her shoulders.

"And you couldn't resist showing us one last time, could you?"

"I want a lawyer," Darva yelled. "All of this is circumstantial. You can't prove any of it!"

"Darva Richmond, I'm arresting you for the murder of Donald Richmond, Sylvia Bennet, and John Jackson. You have the right to remain silent. If you forfeit that right, anything you say can be used against you—"

"You were lucky that wasn't a real weapon," one of the federal marshals told Sharyn.

Sharyn smiled. "I have faith in the security system, I guess."

Epilogue

The night Sharyn had dreaded for so long was finally upon her. The gold dress was brassy enough even for her mother's taste. Sharyn slipped on her gold shoes and picked up her gold shawl that had been a last-minute gift from her mother to both of her daughters.

As usual, she was running late. Kristie and her mother were already at the party. Sharyn had gone to the arraignment for Darva Richmond. Judge White had refused bond and bound her over for three murders. Nick had found strychnine in the real Donald Richmond's body. Reporters had lined the stairs and the sidewalk around the courthouse. Sharyn had avoided the press. The new ADA was suddenly in the spotlight. She watched Jack Winter step into his limousine and be driven away from the back of the courthouse, unnoticed. She knew Caison Talbot was waiting to include his remarks to the press with his own gala affair that night.

Herb Bennet and his wife had been in the courtroom. Their faces had the lost devastation she'd seen on so many others when they learned that a loved one had been killed.

She supposed she must have looked the same when her father died. Her heart went out to them.

She'd hurried home to change for the party. She knew Nick wasn't far behind her.

Dewey was just about to lock up the house as he was leaving. "Sharyn!" The handyman said when he saw her. "I got that pipe fixed. It's a big night for your mother, huh?"

"Yeah. A really big night, Dewey." She smiled at the man she'd known all of her life. "Thanks for coming. Did Mom pay you?"

"She certainly did! And she looked like a queen!" He took in her appearance in the brown sheriff's uniform. "Aren't you going to the party?"

"As soon as I can change, Dewey."

"But not alone?" he speculated, glancing at the driveway that was empty except for her Jeep.

"Not alone," she agreed with a smile. "Thanks again."

"Next time," he offered a word of wisdom, "don't try to do it yourself, huh?"

"I won't," she promised, then hurried inside to get dressed.

Her nervous hands fumbled with the zipper on her dress and refused to work on buttons. Her hair had another plan from the one she'd given it and one of her new earrings broke while she was trying to put it on. She looked at herself in the mirror. The gold wasn't bad on her. Her mother had been right about that.

She was as nervous as someone . . . on a first date. *It isn't a date*, she argued with her reflection. It was . . .

The doorbell rang and she dropped her lipstick on the floor. She ran to answer the door. Nick stood on the step, tall and dark and handsome in a black tux. Her heart stopped beating, then resumed at a rapid pace.

"You look great," he said with a slow, appreciative smile. His eyes were pinned to her face. "Ready?"

"Yes," she replied, feeling both confident and giddy. She took a step forward and dropped her gold purse on the floor at her feet. They both scrambled to pick up what fell out and the phone rang from the cabinet behind Sharyn. She glanced at it and bit her lip.

"Go ahead. You know you don't have any choice. If they want you bad enough, they'll send the National Guard for you." He watched her as she smiled then picked up the phone. Her face went pale and all of the sparkle that had been in her bright blue eyes disappeared. "What's wrong?"

Sharyn put down the phone and shook her head, trying to get control of her emotions.

"Sharyn?" he asked, taking her hand.

"Trudy's husband, Ben. He was just killed in a pile up at the racetrack. She ran down to try to get to him but he was dead before she could reach him." She closed her eyes. Nick's hand tightened on hers. Her fingers held his.

Outside, a long, black limousine slipped down the street, past her house.